KNOTTED BY THE WOLF PRINCE

FURRY ALIEN MATES
BOOK 1

DELANEY RAIN

KNOTTED BY THE WOLF PRINCE © 2023 by Delaney Rain

All rights reserved.

No part of this book may be reproduced in any form or by any electronic or mechanical means, including information storage and retrieval systems, without written permission from the author, except for the use of brief quotations in a book review.

Cover design by Delaney Rain Author Services. Any person depicted on the cover is a model.

Formatting by Delaney Rain Author Services

NO AI/NO BOT. I do not consent to any Artificial Intelligence (AI), generative AI, large language model, machine learning, chatbot, or other automated analysis, generative process, or replication program to reproduce, mimic, remix, summarize, or otherwise replicate any part of this creative work, via any means: print, graphic, sculpture, multimedia, audio, or other medium. I support the right of humans to control their artistic works.

Knot Icon by Kick from The Noun Project (CC BY 3.0)

With thanks to Tammy, Nicole, and Trace for their collective advice and eagle eyes.

*For all of the members of the
Queer Monster Sanctuary Facebook Group.*

GLOSSARY

These are the races of Norlons as they refer to themselves and how humans interpret those names:

- Pip = anthropomorphic rabbits
- Yook = anthro wolves
- Khess = anthro felines
- Cero = anthro lizards
- Beku = anthro otters
- Lago = anthro foxes

PROLOGUE
OFFICER LOGAN PARRISH

Two days. I'd been an officer with the Cleveland Police Department for all of two damn days when a real live spaceship meandered past the moon, heading straight for Earth. I'd wanted to hunker down in my apartment in front of the TV with a tinfoil hat on my head, but instead, I'd had to report for duty and ride out the panic with the rest of my fellow officers. Or at least with the ones who hadn't run for the hills to join the preppers or packed into the churches to pray through the end of the world. I'd quelled more riots and fighting than I ever cared to see again in just the first forty-eight hours.

When the United Nations released video of the aliens explaining why they were there a week later, things had calmed down enough for me to take off my riot gear. I could've slept, but no way could I take my eyes off the screen as creatures that looked like animals but talked like people. Anthropomorphic animals as aliens wasn't something anyone had thought to expect.

Well, except for the Furry community. Those people

were fucking ecstatic that we weren't being visited by little green men but by wolves, tigers, foxes, and whatnot that walked on two legs and were smarter than any human being I'd ever known. And, yeah, after devouring every bit of information I could get my hands on about them, I was definitely seeing the appeal of big, strong, hairy guys.

And then a month into things, we found out our city would be hosting the aliens' first official visit. Of all the fucking places on the entire Earth and they chose *Cleveland*? It could've been one of the great mysteries of the universe, but the head alien, a prince who looked like a wolf, had freely admitted that his stepdad had been a human man abducted from Ohio by actual little green men. After the panic of that giant ball of *the fuck did he just say?* died down, we came to understand the prince had loved his mother's mate like family, respected him in every way, and was honoring the man's memory by meeting humans in the place where he'd been born. It was kinda sweet. Carl Iger's relatives had been flabbergasted and were now living it up on their fifteen minutes of fame.

But I was still one damn month on the force when my city was set to host aliens.

I was also not at all someone who was on the inside of any logistical discussion whatsoever and barely got told more than where I was going to stand for the foreseeable future. Never, not once, had I thought I might see one of the aliens off in the distance, let alone get anywhere near being able to touch one.

I definitely never thought I'd tackle one in order to foil an assassination attempt.

CHAPTER 1
PRINCE ALAM YE LENA

Humans were strange creatures. Even living with one as I grew into adulthood hadn't afforded me any greater insight into their minds than the other members of the delegation possessed from mere passing acquaintance. As we walked down the shuttle's ramp and into the presence of thousands of humans for only the second time since our arrival in their solar system, it was becoming clear that there were two camps amongst them: those who welcomed us wholeheartedly, and those who cautiously tolerated our presence.

Some of the humans were here as protection and so wore expressions of seriousness as they watched us and the civilians surrounding them in equal measure. Others were desperate to keep their faces neutral—no doubt so that they might appear as though our meeting did not trouble them at all—but the sour scent of their fear was hard to miss.

And then there were the humans in the back who were dressed to look like us in furry costumes. Earth had a myriad of primitive non-sentient species that resembled us, so it was interesting that these humans had developed a subculture elevating those animals to our level before they even knew we existed. I could admit to liking them best of all, so when I raised a hand and waved to the crowd, I was truly waving at them. Their enthusiastic reaction made me laugh quietly and feel like I was beloved in ways merely being a prince of my people had never provided.

Beside me, Administrator Rijal growled before saying, "Why can we not negotiate with the lovers? They would happily give us anything we wanted."

Thankfully, he spoke in Norlish so the humans nearest us could not understand him, and I spoke the same as I admonished him. "Hush, Ghosha. Remember, we are not here to take."

He laughed, brief and sharp, golden eyes scanning the crowd and long, white whiskers twitching. The humans called him a tiger and me a wolf. Cats, canines, they classified us in their own ways regardless of how many times we told them what we called ourselves. When they prefaced those labels with the word anthropomorphic... It was disappointing that they could only understand us in terms of them, but it was a start, so I tried not to let it frustrate me.

"You may be here to give," Ghosha said, "but my entire purpose as a member of this delegation is to take and take and *take*."

I watched as he smoothed his whiskers across one black and white striped cheek and licked the cleft in his upper lip while grinning just enough to reveal one fang. The human woman he'd aimed that at gasped a breath and pressed a hand to her chest as her blue eyes widened and face flushed. Her lust suddenly perfumed the air as we walked past her.

I resisted rolling my eyes at his flirting. "Do try to keep it in your pants for a bit longer. We have barely scratched the surface of sexuality and compatibility with them. They were entirely shocked by the anatomy information we gave them and that was done via drawings alone."

We each had our specialties, and Ghosha was here to lead the committee working toward bringing humans to Nor so they might work in our thriving sex industry. The committee I lead was responsible for everything from the first contact we had achieved last month to our overall goals as one society integrating with another. Since we were all familiar with humans due to the vast number of them that we Norlons had rescued decades ago from the Vigzek—a devious people of small stature and green skin bent on treating humans as chattel—we had taken the advice of our human advisors to begin by explaining to the Earth humans the most basic information of what made us Norlon.

Which was when we had learned about the wonderful subculture of humans that called themselves Furries. Unfortunately, the man who had explained that to us had been hastily and forcibly removed from the room, so we understood now that it was not a widely accepted view. But Ghosha was right; he should have a very easy time of recruitment if he approached the Furries. We would be inundated with volunteers, and the brothels and their patrons back home would be ecstatic.

The rest of humanity was not at all excited to know that

we Norlons enjoyed an open and free view of sexual relations between our great variety of peoples and genders. Some humans had entire belief systems built around chastity and purity that made no sense to us, but it did not preclude us from respecting their choices. The differences of opinion, however, could become quite the sticking point during negotiations if we did not tread carefully. Hence my cautioning Ghosha.

Wrangling the high-ranking members of the delegation was also my responsibility.

An intriguing scent caught my attention and had me sniffing the air while I continued walking toward the building. I'd thought I knew most of the scents associated with human emotions, but this one was new to me. It didn't smell artificial like so many of their added fragrances did and it… Well, it was rather arousing.

A moment later and a human in black clothing and a strange round hat turned and ran toward me. He yelled a single word—one I wasn't familiar with—and launched himself into my arms. I caught him easily and just seconds before I heard a rapid succession of small explosions and some sort of tiny projectiles impacted against his back and his hat.

Shrinking away in confusion and fear, I clutched the human to my chest as he went limp against me. My guards immediately closed rank around us, and I quickly found myself caught up in the wave of Norlons rushing back to the shuttle.

Had the human in my arms saved me from those projectiles?

I cradled him close and ran with everyone else as the

other humans in the crowd and their dignitaries scattered around us. Within seconds I was running up the ramp and into the shuttle.

I was exceedingly grateful that our security teams coordinated a headcount and check of everyone's welfare as I was entirely unable to do more than hold the human in my arms and gasp for breath.

"What happened?" I asked as they finally closed the shuttle and the engines roared to life. "Rampon?"

Sergeant Rampon Molwynog, head of my security, said, "I believe that was an assassination attempt, Your Highness. The human there must have seen the attacker first. Is he alive?"

"Goddess bless," I whispered as I loosed my grip on him and gazed down at his bloody face. "I… I don't…"

"Your Highness." Doctor Halaby Revazi, another member of the delegation, came over to me. "Let's set him down so I can examine him."

"And I need to search him," Rampon said sternly.

"Search him?" I held the warm body of my protector closer. "For what?"

"Weapons and explosive devices."

"What?" My anger spiked. "I cannot believe someone who would *sacrifice himself* to protect me could also be a threat to me."

"Please, Your Highness. I must insist." Rampon held out his scaled hands toward me.

I looked to Halaby, suddenly terrified that if I let the human go, he would die.

"It's alright, Your Highness." Halaby gave me a small, understanding smile and cradled the human's head. "Just set him down on his chest. I'll help."

My hands shook as I gave in and gently maneuvered the unconscious human around in my arms. My assistant Bashtine removed her cloak and settled it on the floor, a move I appreciated as I lowered the human on top of it. When she stepped back, I made myself do the same. Halaby stayed kneeling beside the human, and Rampon worked around him.

Rampon found several items attached to the human's thick belt and simply removed it from him. "This is a projectile weapon called a gun," Rampon said to me and pointed at it. "I don't recognize these, but their close proximity to the gun makes me think they may also be weaponry."

I sighed. "I apologize, Sergeant. Thank you for insisting."

"Quite alright, sir. I don't consider him a threat, but it's best that we keep these items secure while he's with us."

"Fascinating," Halaby murmured as he poked around in the holes in the human's garment. "His clothing seems to have stopped the projectiles." He held up a flattened bit of metal.

I knelt on the other side of the human. "So he is not injured? Well, not as badly as first thought?" I amended since his face was still covered in blood and he remained unconscious.

"It's possible his facial injury is due to the projectile impacting the back of his projective hat," Halaby said, pointing, "which forced his head forward, causing his face to strike your breastplate."

I gasped as I looked down and realized the human's

blood was indeed all over the emblem of my people that decorated the very center of my breastplate. Feeling horrible to have caused him harm, I reached behind myself and tore the fastenings free. Bashtine was there to take the whole thing away.

While I'd done that, Halaby and Rampon had managed to remove the human's hat and vest. I couldn't help the concerned whine that left my throat upon seeing the two deep purple bruises on his back. So, though the projectiles had not penetrated his delicate skin, they *had* hurt him. The back of his head was blessedly uninjured.

Halaby scanned the human's head and back with one of his medical devices, dark brows drawn low over his yellow eyes as he read the readings. "Bruising and a broken nasal bridge bone seem to be the extent of his injuries."

"Why is he unconscious?"

"The sudden impact to his face. There's no brain damage or facial fracturing other than his nose." Halaby patted my hand. "I'm sure he'll awaken soon."

"And you can heal him, yes?"

"Oh, definitely." Halaby stowed the device back into his bag. "However, as he doesn't have anything critically wrong, I'd prefer to wait for his consent before treating him."

I nodded even though I didn't want him to awaken in the pain he would no doubt feel. "We will take him to the infirmary and…and…" I sputtered to a stop as I realized I had no idea what might come next.

"I have already alerted my team, Your Highness," Halaby said kindly. "They will meet us in the landing bay to transport him to the infirmary. Don't worry."

I took a deep breath and tried to calm myself only to realize that intriguing scent from before was coming from my rescuer. It wasn't an emotion he was feeling since he was unconscious, and it wasn't something he'd put on either. The scent was just…him.

It made me want to hold him again.

The shuttle bumped as it landed within the ship. Only then did I realized that I had just perpetrated an abduction.

CHAPTER 2
LOGAN

I opened my eyes because I couldn't figure out why I was on a rollercoaster, only to discover I was actually on a gurney. Someone was rolling me through a brightly lit room until I bumped into a wall. That might not have been so weird except for the fact that everyone around me was definitely not human.

"Hello." Above me was a person with a round, furry face, triangular brown nose, and big black eyes. He reminded me of an otter. "I'm glad you're awake."

"What…" I caught sight of a hell of a lot of symbols scrolling or blinking on the wall above my head and lost my train of thought for a second. "Um… What's going on?"

"I'm Doctor Halaby Revazi. You're in my infirmary. Can you tell me your name?"

"Logan Parrish." I tried to sit up but holy fuck my back hurt.

"Stay where you are, Logan. You were hit with metal projectiles—"

"Bullets," another alien said. That one looked like a leopard.

"Ah, thank you," the doctor said to them with a nod. "Your vest stopped the bullets, but—"

"Yeah, okay," I said as I remembered. "I got in front of them and…" I trailed off and winced as my nose made itself known. "Did I hit my head, too?"

"You were struck in the back and the head. Your garments stopped the bullets, but the one that hit your head snapped you forward into the prince's breastplate. Your nose is—"

I grabbed the doctor's arm. "The prince! Is he okay?"

"Yes," he said and patted my hand. I released him as he said, "He's right here."

The black-furred wolf prince came closer and leaned over me. "Are you well?" he asked urgently. "I sincerely apologize for your nose."

I tried to smile, but my nose and eyes felt swollen. "I'll live. How—"

He cut me off with a very canine whine of distress that sliced through the room as he cupped my chin in one big, soft-skinned palm. "Your poor face. And those bullets could have killed you!"

I shivered at the gentle touch of his velvety fingertips as I looked up at him. "Yeah, they could've, but I had my gear on. I really am alright." He gazed at me with blue eyes that were full of worry and maybe a little guilt, so I said, "It's not your fault. Regardless of what people think of you Norlods being here, nobody has a right to try to kill you."

I was aware of the fringe groups that had sprung up almost overnight when the aliens made themselves known.

Something called Humans First was gaining a hell of a lot of followers who wanted the aliens to leave and never come back. I had to wonder if the Fed who'd tried to kill the prince had been a member. Could more be lurking out there, waiting to pounce?

One corner of the prince's mouth twitched as he withdrew his hand from my cheek. "Norlons," he corrected.

"Oh, yeah, sorry." I clicked my tongue at myself. "Norlons."

"I appreciate your willingness to defend us."

"Yeah, of course, Your Highness."

"Alam."

"Sorry?" I didn't know that word, but I also noticed that everyone nearly snapped their necks to look at the prince like he'd said something surprising.

"It's my name," he said with a smile. "Alam Ye Lena. Please call me Alam."

"Oh, okay." That was odd, right? Calling a royal by his first name? Well, maybe it wasn't for them. "It's nice to actually meet you, Alam. So, um… Did someone catch the guy?"

Alam cocked his wolfish head at me. "What guy?"

"The shooter? He looked like one of the Feds— Uh, Federal Bureau of Investigations agents. Did someone stop—"

"Rampon?" Alam looked behind him, and I tried not to react as a giant lizard stepped closer to us. It seemed like these scaly, green-gray dudes made up most of the alien security team, and I thought that was fitting. I had to wonder if their hides really were as tough as they looked since they were covered in small shields. Like could they stop a bullet without a vest?

"I don't have that information, Your Highness," Rampon said in a voice that rivaled thunder, "but I can request it from the humans."

"Yes, please do. Please also let them know that we won't be returning until they provide better protection for everyone involved. If this attacker was one of them…" Alam shook his head and sighed. "I will not risk our lives simply because they want proper media coverage of us."

"That's why?" I blurted. When all eyes were suddenly on me, I waved their attention away. "Sorry. I just wondered why they made you walk so far out in the open like that."

Rampon had pink eyes and his sudden focused attention pinned me to the spot. "We were assured that the only humans who would have weapons were their own security teams, like you, and that the exposure was to reassure the human public as to our peaceful intentions. They called it transparency."

"Well, that's fine, but with the threats—"

"Threats?"

I blinked at him, suddenly feeling like I was giving away secrets. But also I couldn't believe no one had told them. "Humans First? And other groups, but that's the big one, I think. If no one told you about them, that's a problem. *They're* a problem."

"They haven't," he said on a growl. "Your Highness, I must insist on access to the humans' data streams. I understand that they deserve their privacy, but if they aren't giving us the full picture—"

"Permission granted. Bashtine?" Alam said, and a brown

wolf who looked far more feminine than the prince approached him. "Speak to Tech for the necessary access, then coordinate with Rampon who should have the information."

"Yes, Your Highness," she said and focused her attention on a tablet in her hands as she stepped back.

"Thank you, Your Highness." Rampon bobbed his head at the prince, but his gaze was still on me like he had a lot more questions. He moved out of my line of sight with the brown wolf—Bashtine—and I refocused on the prince.

"I apologize," Alam said, "but if the humans aren't providing us with information related to our security, then we must discover it by any means necessary."

I shrugged only to wince as it pulled on my back. "I figured you all were already scanning us or whatever. I mean, I would be if our roles were reversed. Plenty of people are cool with you being here—me included—but others really aren't."

Alam smiled at me, and I felt the lightly furred fingers brushed my hand. I couldn't help the shiver of awareness that went through me at his touch.

"Sergeant Molwynog may have additional questions for you," Alam said. "Would that be acceptable? After your actions to save me, I believe you are an ally we can trust."

"Oh, yeah, I am. I meant what I said. Folks can disagree and protest or whatever, but violence? No way."

"Excellent."

I felt his fingers again, this time almost petting me, and swallowed hard as way more than awareness cascaded through me. Was this wolf-like prince flirting with me?

"If I may, Your Highness?" the doctor asked and waggled an ampule of something clear at him.

"Oh. Yes, of course."

The prince stepped back as the doctor said, "Logan, I have here enough nanobots to heal your injuries in under an hour. Would you allow me to inject them into your body?"

"Oh. Um…" I gulped. He wanted to inject alien tech into me?

He smiled kindly. "I can answer any questions you have about them."

"Um, they're safe for me, right? Like, have you ever used them on a human before?"

"Absolutely," he said with a smile. "We don't have many humans on Nor, but one of the first things we did when they arrived was adjust our medical technology to include them. These nanobots are specifically for human use."

I probably should've asked more questions, but the only thing I could think about then was how I'd be able to get back to work faster if I let him use those things on me. Otherwise, I'd be off work while I recovered, and I had no idea how long that could be. I'd have to apply for worker's compensation, too, and who knew how long that would take to come through for the new guy. I just wanted to get back to normal as fast as possible, and if those nanobots would let that happen, well…

"Okay," I said. "Let's do it."

The otter doctor and his leopard nurse prepared a syringe, and then he injected it into my upper arm. Aside from the sting of the needle, I didn't feel a thing. I expected to feel something—like, there were microscopic robots inside me, shouldn't I feel them crawling around or vibrating? But there was nothing at all—which was good because I didn't want to feel like there were bugs inside me.

"I'd like to clean you up," the nurse said and showed me a packet of what looked like wet wipes. "Is that alright?"

I probably could've gotten the dried blood off myself, but I didn't really want to move much while the bots were inside me. "Sure, yeah. Thank you."

"If I may?" Alam asked as he stepped closer. "I'd like to speak with Logan a bit more."

"Oh." She looked to me, eyebrows raised.

For some reason, that he wanted to be the one to wash me made me blush, but I said, "Sure, that's fine."

The nurse handed the wipes off to the prince and switched places with him.

"I feel responsible for this," Alam said as he gently dabbed beside my nose.

"It's not your fault."

Interestingly, it didn't hurt when he touched my nose even though it probably should've. Was that the nanobots dulling the pain while they fixed me up? The pressure was lessening, like maybe the swelling was going down. That was crazy fast.

Alam shrugged. "Perhaps not, but I still wish to find ways that I may repay you."

Why was him wiping blood from my face turning me on? It wasn't exactly an erotic sensation. He wasn't using his tongue, for Pete's sake. There was a lot of eye contact, though. He had really beautiful blue eyes. And, dammit, I was actually getting hard like some kind of hormonal teenager. I gulped in embarrassment and tried not to squirm.

"Thank you, Logan," he said, his voice damn near a purr.

"Hmm?" I cleared my throat. "What'd you say?"

He grinned and kept carefully swiping at my face. "For your bravery and quick reflexes. No one else knew what was happening, but you did."

"Oh, yeah, of course." I shrugged and it didn't hurt this time. "But others saw. They were already moving when I yelled."

"You saw *first* and that is why…" He trailed off, clearly hesitating.

I was too curious not to ask, "What's why what?"

He frowned at me. "What?"

I huffed a laugh. Yeah, and I was the native English speaker here. "What were you going to say?"

"Ah," he said with a chuckle. "I wondered if it might be advantageous for us both if you were to join my security detail."

While Alam was talking, I could almost forget that he was an alien that looked like a wolf. But seeing his teeth when he laughed brought it back. And he wanted *me* to protect him? Sure, he was some kind of royalty, but he looked like he could tear a person apart with his bare hands, maybe bite their head off, too. The guards that had been with him had been a mix of wolf and lizard ones, so why— "Why would want me when you've got all of those badass dudes already guarding you? Is it the vests? You had on a metal thing earlier. What's it made of? Maybe those are enough to stop bullets."

They all wore corset-like garments with symbols on them that covered their torsos, but maybe they weren't as metallic as they looked. Just because whacking into one with my face had broken my nose didn't mean the things could stop a bullet.

"There!" he said with a big smile. "You're already assisting me. When you join my security detail, you can test our metals against your bullets."

It sounded like an opportunity of a lifetime, but... "What happens when... I mean, are you staying here forever? Will you go back to, um, Nor at some point?"

"Yes, the plan is that I will return home eventually. Hopefully having successfully joined our peoples together in as many ways as possible for our mutual benefits," he said with a grin. That faded as he blinked down at me. "You would have the choice to accompany me, or remain here on another's security team. Additional opportunities may present themselves in human circles after you gain this experience as well."

I nodded since he had a good point there. But leave Earth for Nor? Damn, that was tempting, too. Because it wasn't a leave forever kind of situation since their ships could make the trip back and forth just fine. They had faster-than-light engines that had us all referencing every space movie ever made to explain them. I had no doubt that traveling between our planets would someday become as easy as going to a different country was now. Exploring an alien planet sounded so very cool.

"Can I have some time to think about it? It's really tempting, but I want to make sure I know what I'm getting into, you know?"

"Absolutely." Alam traded one wipe for another and moved down to my chin and neck. "We can discuss everything in detail once you're healed. Rampon will be an excellent resource for you as well."

"Oh, yeah, okay." I tipped my chin up to give him more room at my throat and felt a shiver snake through me for some reason. "You all deserve to know what's going on so you can be prepared. It's not right that they didn't tell you about the anti-Norlon groups popping up. And I get that you didn't want to be invasive or whatever with our computer systems and stuff like that, but at least watch the news. They're covering all of that and more."

"See?" he said with a grin. "We need you, Logan. The humans that have accompanied us here to Earth were abducted back before your digital capabilities were as they are now. They've been fascinated by what's available and interested in delving into it—as has Security—but it felt far too invasive to tap in uninvited."

"I'm glad you've changed your stance on it," I said and my voice sounded breathless. The way he was gently swiping at my neck... Fuck, he might as well be licking me because it felt that intimate.

"There," Alam said and stood up straight. "Once you're recovered, you can wash properly, but now you look much better. The spots on your skin are visible again."

I chuckled. "My freckles?"

He cocked his head at me, grinning. "Are they everywhere?"

"Well, anywhere I get exposed to the sun." Why did that make me blush?

Alam touched my upper arm, giving me a light squeeze.

"Why don't you rest? Recover. I need to check in with everyone, so I'll reconnect with you soon."

"Sure, okay."

I couldn't resist watching him walk away, but the robe thing he wore didn't let me see much. Except for his tail. It was long, black, and looked incredibly soft. It swished back and forth as he walked out of the room. I gulped and closed my eyes, trying to regain some composure.

"That's normal," the nurse said.

I opened my eyes to see her grinning at me. "Normal?"

"He's a *very* fine male."

A laugh jumped out of me, and my face flamed hot. She patted my shoulder and checked the IV thing and whatever was happening with the panel on the wall over my head. So, I wasn't at all subtle about my response to the prince if my nurse knew. But did Alam know?

CHAPTER 3
ALAM

I had to have him. Logan's desire had filled my senses as I'd cleaned him, making me wish we could've been alone so I that may have given in to the temptation he presented. That we weren't alone, that he was still injured, were the only reasons I hadn't tried to woo him. The musky male scent of his need had my head spinning and the rest of me wishing for a private room and just a few minutes alone. My cock ached for want of Logan.

But I had duties to attend to, like finding out what had happened after we left Earth and what should take place now. I truly had thought resisting the temptation of watching the humans' every broadcast was the polite thing to do, allowing their leaders to inform us of their people's reactions and desires. But if they weren't being honest about the level of the threats against us, then we needed to do whatever possible to learn the truth and take steps to protect ourselves.

I dearly hoped the situation was not so terrible that we would be forced to leave entirely. If necessary, I would do so, but I didn't want to abandon the mission. There was so much we could do for each other if they could come to accept us.

Walking toward the lift, I spoke to Bashtine, who I could always count on to be nearby. "Is everyone assembled in the conference room?"

"They are, Your Highness."

"How are they fairing?" I felt badly for how I'd ignored them in favor of seeing to Logan's health. "None were injured, correct?"

"Correct, sir. Several members of the delegation are shaken by the experience, and all of them have requested that we not return to the planet's surface without additional protections in place. Administrator Rijal mentioned using a Benendal forcefield."

I huffed a laugh at the idea of us walking through a tube of energy normally reserved for prisoner transport. But then I had to wonder if that might be a good idea. "I'll consider it," I told her.

Rampon stepped up beside me. "Your Highness, I've only had access to the humans' broadcasts for a limited amount of time, but the news is already disturbing."

Disappointment had my shoulders slumping. "Have they at least apprehended the one responsible for the attack?"

"Unfortunately, sir, another member of the human security teams killed him. However, the threat to the delegation is a great deal bigger than one person."

It disturbed me that the attacker couldn't be questioned and rehabilitated, that violence had been met with more violence, and that our presence was causing so much of it.

"So are things as Logan said? Are there factions of humans acting against us?"

"There are, sir." His normally bright pink eyes were dull, a clear sign of his upset. "A group calling themselves Humans First has claimed responsibility for the attack and promised additional retribution if we do not leave Earth."

"Leave entirely?" I asked in disbelief as we reached the lift that would take us to the conference room. The three of us entered, and Rampon chose our destination. "No negotiations for additional resources or knowledge? Just… leave?"

"Yes, sir. Humans First is an accurate name as that is their only goal: humans before all others. They claim this planet is theirs, that we are invading and threatening their way of life, and that we must be removed at all costs. They speak in terms of war."

"Goddess," I whispered, incredibly saddened. "Thank you, Sergeant. Please continue to learn all you can and…" I shook my head, hating what I needed to say. "Prepare your guard to meet all threats as though we *are* at war. I do not want us caught by surprise again."

"Understood, Your Highness." Rampon focused on his tablet device, no doubt spreading the word to his guards.

"Have we heard from any of the humans in authority?" I was being deliberately vague since so many of the human leaders claimed to be the one in charge of them all.

"Yes, sir," Bashtine answered as the lift stopped and we stepped out. "Several have reached out with promises to investigate and assure our next visit will be without incident. None have been able to express how that might happen specifically, though."

I was sighing as we approached the conference room doors, and two guards opened them for us. Within the expansive room were those members of the delegation that had accompanied me to the surface as well as their personal assistants and several more guards. They quieted as I stepped up to the end of the table.

"I would like to apologize to all of you," I said sincerely. "I was ill-prepared for the threat against us and put each of you in danger." My tail drooped low as I resisted the urge to tuck it between my legs in shame. "Should you wish to elect another to replace me, I will step aside."

A few gasped, and others shook their heads as Ghosha said, "Nonsense! None of us were prepared for such violence, so none of us could've done a better job. I say you maintain your position."

Heartened by his confidence in me, I looked to each of them as they added their agreements.

Relieved, I touched my chest over my heart in gratitude. "Thank you."

Putting that aside, I gave the floor to Rampon so that he could explain what he knew about Humans First. Hopefully, we would be able to come to some kind of decision on how to proceed with everyone's input.

Since he was still on my mind, I leaned close to Bashtine and asked her to send someone to escort Logan to my quarters once he was well enough to leave the infirmary. I wanted to speak with him again and see if he might accept my offer of employment. Clearly, we needed him.

Several hours later, I entered my quarters alone and with a desperate desire to change clothes and escape my duties for as long as possible. It wasn't that things weren't going well—they were—but the emotional toll of the entire day was dragging on me, and I needed a break. I went directly to my closet, selected a pair of comfortable trousers, and began removing my ceremonial robes.

"Uh, Alam? Your Highness?"

Robes around my waist, I clutched them there and turned to see Logan getting up from a chair in the sitting area. I was flooded by sudden embarrassment at overlooking his presence so completely. And only now did I catch his intriguing scent.

He waved awkwardly. "I thought I should stop you before you went too much further there. I didn't realize you didn't see me until now."

I flipped my robes back up. "I apologize, Logan. I was so absorbed in myself that I saw nothing else."

"No, it's okay. And you can go ahead and change." He turned his back to me. "I'm not looking."

"Thank you." I did want out of the stuffy clothes, so I continued to undress. The intimacy of the act with him right there wasn't lost on me. Neither was the fact that he was healed completely. "You look well. May I assume the doctor has proclaimed you fully restored?"

He nodded. "Yeah, I'm good now. No pain anywhere." He chuckled as he said, "I'm pretty sure those nanobots fixed up an old knee injury while they were in there. And did you know I'll end up, uh… To get them out, um…"

I smiled as I put on my trousers, guessing he was trying to find a polite way to say he would eventually eliminate the nanobots from his body through urination. "I know how they leave the body."

He laughed quietly. "I almost feel bad that they've got such a short lifespan, but also it's like there's all these microscopic dead bodies floating inside me."

I coughed to cover up the snort that slipped out of me. "That *is* a horrible thought. Thinking of them as robots isn't much improved, though." Barefooted, I left the closet and walked into the kitchenette. "Would you like something to eat or drink?"

When he didn't answer, I looked over to see him staring at me. Or more specifically, at my body. Perhaps I shouldn't have gone without a tunic, or chosen less form-fitting pants, but I also couldn't help enjoying his heated gaze. Logan Parrish liked what he could see of me.

His eyes flicked up and widened as he realized I'd caught him, a blush quickly staining his cheeks. I grinned with roguish satisfaction at the scent of his desire slithering through the air.

Logan cleared his throat. "Um, what?"

"Are you hungry? Thirsty?" I asked again and turned to face him fully.

His pink lips parted as he gasped a tiny breath, his gaze fixed below my waist. I couldn't suppress how my tail needed to sway to express my delight for his clear interest in how well-endowed I was. He looked up at my face and a grin broke across his before he glanced away and laughed.

"Don't worry, Logan, I enjoy your attention. You have mine as well."

He nodded, his blush still bright. "Okay. Um… Thank you."

Rather than ask for a third time if he wanted anything, I gathered up a few items and brought them over to the sitting area. He waited until I'd sat down before he did, and I realized he still wore quite a bit of his black uniform.

"Did no one offer you a change of clothes?" I looked about for the tablet that would allow me to message any number of people.

"Oh, they did. I just…wasn't sure what was next."

I nodded, understanding. "We did leave things unresolved, didn't we? I apologize." I was saying that a lot today. "I should have saved discussing the possibilities for when I was able to truly talk through everything with you."

"It's alright. I've had plenty of time to talk to some other people in the infirmary. And then Kevin, the human who brought me here, had a lot to say, too."

"Ah, Kevin," I said with a smile. "He is a wonderful human."

"He's hilarious. Told me all about getting abducted like twenty years ago and ending up on Nor after the rescue, and somehow made me laugh about it with him. I can't remember what he called the bad aliens, but he couldn't say enough about how great Norlons have been."

I picked up a glass and took a sip, my family's ale easing me as much as Logan's willingness to accept me. Us, actually. That he was accepting of Norlons as a whole was a balm on my day. "I'm glad to hear that," I told him.

Logan picked up his own glass and sniffed it. With a smile, he took a healthy swallow. "So, um, will you all be going back down to the planet any time soon?"

"Ah, goddess," I groaned and leaned forward. "Logan, I must apologize again because only after we arrived did I realize I had stolen you away for your entire world. If you wish to go back immediately—"

"No!" His blush brightened as he pulled back the hand he'd thrust out at me. "I just meant that I hope you're not going to leave. That what happened today wasn't, like, the last straw. You know? I'm not upset that you brought me here and got me this level of medical care. Not at all."

I relaxed again and took another drink. "We have not yet decided if returning to the surface is in our best interest." Though Logan had not yet accepted my offer of employment, it didn't feel wrong to trust him with more information. "Those amongst the human leadership that we've spoken to were apologetic and eager to assist in any way necessary to repair relations. Some seemed sincere. Some…did not." I waved that away since a solution to determining their sincerity was in process. "Rampon has dedicated an entire platoon to investigating these leaders to determine whether they have any affiliation with the opposition groups. We should soon know who is truly for or against our presence."

"Man, I'm sorry. I mean, I knew opinions were all over the place, but I thought that they were just that, opinions. Words. Now that it's assassination attempts…" He bit his bottom lip and shook his head.

"Would you help us? Act as a consultant to guide us as we learn whether our goals are at all possible now?"

Logan looked me in the eyes and nodded. "Yeah, I want to help."

Relief flooded me as I smiled. "Thank you."

"You're welcome. I'm happy to do it." His blush was back.

Part of me wanted to rush to make use of what he knew, gain his every insight, and solve all of our problems as quickly as possible. But seeing his pleased and eager face, the pinkness of it and how his blue eyes shone so brightly, had me wishing to take my time. To make certain Logan stayed and stayed.

CHAPTER 4
LOGAN

Was he flirting with me? Alam could wear whatever he wanted, and I could keep my eyes above his waist, of course. Fuck, he was *hung*. There was a lot— *Eyes up, Parrish!* I felt yet another blush lighting up my face as I snapped my gaze back to his eyes. It was just the *way* he watched me... Man, I had my uniform on and his gaze made me feel naked! The fact that there was a big bed behind me was distracting, too. But I needed to concentrate since I'd basically just changed my entire life in favor of consulting with aliens.

"So, um, what should I do first?" I asked him.

"I imagine we should do several administrative tasks, like establishing your employment with our government and determining your residence." He averted his gaze and sighed before saying, "Or would you prefer to remain on the surface and consult remotely? That is entirely within your rights and our capabilities."

But he didn't want me to—I could see that clearly in the way he asked the question, and it did even more for how much I wanted to straddle his thighs and find out if he knew about kissing. I licked my lips before I realized what I was doing.

"Um, no, I can stay here if there's a place for me. I have an apartment, but no plants or animals I need to take care of, you know? I should go there to pack some clothes and things, but that's it." I grunted a laugh. "I should probably let my superiors know I'm not dead and that I'm quitting."

Alam grinned at me. "That sounds like an especially good place to start. I'm sure Bashtine knows far more than I do about how to integrate you into our communications systems and make you an official member of the delegation. I'll let her know what's happened."

"And Bashtine is the brown, um..." I stalled out, not sure if calling her—and him—a wolf would be offensive.

"Yook," he said. "We are called Yook. Rampon, the head of my security, is a Cero."

"Right, okay." Since we were talking about it, I asked, "And the doctor and nurse?"

"Halaby is a Beku and his nurse is a Khess."

"Is it..." I hesitated. "I hope it isn't offensive, but do you know that you look like a wolf? On Earth, I mean. Like, we have animals that— Not that I think you're an animal!"

"Logan," Alam said with a laugh, "it's not offensive. Are we not all animals? I'm certainly not a plant or a rock. I am sentient, though, so a more evolved animal than some. I know humans have referred to us as anthropomorphic animals in order to relate us to something familiar. I believe that would mean Halaby is an otter, his nurse is a cat—though there are a great variety of those—and the captain of the ship is a fox."

"I'm glad it's not offensive, but you know what? You all might want to look into creating your own website and pamphlets or something so that you can control the information about yourselves that's out there. Like an official resource. Because I've heard all of those names before, but I don't have a permanent reference I can check when I have questions. Everything's filtered through the media outlets." I shrugged. "They could get things wrong."

Alam's expression brightened and he sat up a little more. "That is an excellent idea. Yes, I like that. Are you familiar with how to accomplish such things?"

I cringed. "Uh, no, not really. I mean, I know anyone can make a site, but not the stuff that has to happen so you can. If you've got people who can scour the internet for info, maybe they're tech-savvy enough to figure it out?"

He was nodding and looking around before he stood up and walked over to the door where he'd left his tablet on a side table. I couldn't keep my eyes anywhere but on his muscular ass and the fluffy black tail poking through a hole in his pants. Desire sizzled through me like I'd had a fetish for tails all my life and never realized it. Because it wasn't his ass that I wanted to get my hands on.

Alam wandered back to his chair, head bowed over the tablet as he tapped at the screen. Realizing I wanted to hang onto his tail while now practically eye-level with his bulging dick had me sucking in a deep breath and tearing my gaze away. My imagination was showing me an idea for stroking his tail while deep-throating his cock…

I looked back to him when I heard Alam sniffing. Aw hell, with a nose like his, he could probably smell my every dirty thought as it made my cock throb. But then he grinned at me.

"Don't worry, Logan. I am also intrigued by you." Alam sat down again, and I did not stare between his splayed legs. "But if you wish to remain on a more professional level, I will respect that."

I didn't. Lord help me, I knew I should treat him like my boss—my *royal* boss at that—and do the job with my pants on like a grownup. But I didn't want to.

What came out of my mouth was, "Thanks. That's what we should do," but I wasn't sure which scenario I meant. The one he'd suggested or the one in my head?

Alam nodded and went back to tapping at his tablet, so he must've assumed I meant to keep things professional. It was…disappointing. I vowed right then that if he ever mentioned his interest again, I'd say yes.

"No, sir, I was *not* abducted," I said for the third time. "I was relocated to the nearest medical facility they were aware of with all the speed available to them."

I stood in front of a computer monitor on the wall of my new quarters talking to my captain, the chief of police, the district attorney, and the mayor of Cleveland. It was the single most stressful video call of my life because these were pretty damn powerful people and every last one of them wanted to come after the Norlons—and Alam specifically—for running off with me.

Part of me appreciated their protectiveness, but the rest of me just wanted them to listen for one damn minute.

"And I'm not resigning under any kind of duress or coercion," I continued, "just a desire to provide better assistance to our visitors so that another attack is less likely to happen in the future."

I'd already been asked by DA Connors not to refer to the assassination attempt as an assassination attempt, but I wasn't about to call it "the unfortunate incident" either. And since I was stressed and getting pissed off, my inner queen was coming on out and making me sound like a pompous ass.

"I would prefer that you not call what happened—" Connors began before Chief Stevenson started talking over her.

"Son, how about we put you in for a special assignment, hmm? You won't lose your job or your pension, and you can come on back whenever this is over." Stevenson smiled like a crocodile. "Then you can help us while you help them and we can all get through this a little easier."

Why did everything he said make it sound like aliens being here was just some kind of temporary inconvenience? Not to mention turning me into a double agent.

"No, thank you, sir." I was still trying to be polite but for god's sake, they were all getting on my nerves. "This isn't an us versus them situation. We should all be working together for the betterment of everyone."

"See that there?" Stevenson said, pointing at me. "You sound like a radical. Whatever they've done to you, son, I'm sure it's not permanent. Just go along with whatever they tell you. Get them to bring you down here to check on your sick mom or something, and we'll get you to safety."

The fuck? "Did you miss the part about them wanting to cure diseases and open up trade?" I snapped, losing patience. I was quitting, after all, so the gloves could come off. "Like, do you even see that they have tech that can heal a broken nose in an hour? Imagine what else they could do for us!"

"And what will we have to pay?" he asked, leaning closer to the camera. "You go on and ask this prince fellow what it is he wants from us and see if they're really the side you want to be on."

Okay, that sounded bad and since the chief of police was a hell of a lot higher up than I was on the ladder of knowing stuff, I hesitated, wondering what he could mean. "What have they asked for?"

"Stop scaring the boy, Lloyd," Mayor Jacoby said gruffly. "Neither of us have been in those meetings, so don't act like you know anything but rumors and people talking out their asses. You sound like one of those Humans First fuckwads. Don't make me retire you."

Stevenson made a face like he'd eaten a lemon, but he stopped talking. I tried not to laugh by coughing along with Connors and Captain Lewis.

"Logan," Lewis said, "how about an open-ended leave of absence? Then you can consult as long as you need to without resigning your position."

Reassured by Jacoby and grateful to Lewis, I nodded. Maybe I wouldn't need to return to regular police work after consulting for aliens, but that the job would be there for me was nice. "That sounds perfect, thanks."

"And if you run into any issues the department can help with," Lewis added, "please let me know."

Did Lewis add a little extra emphasis to that me at the end there? Sounded like it on my end. "Yes, sir. Thank you again."

"Alright then," Jacoby said. "Do good out there, kid."

"I'll do my best, sir."

"Just a minute—" Stevenson blustered, but Jacoby laughed and cut his connection. I followed suit and ended the call, probably kicking the rest of them off, too.

I felt like such a rebel. I also felt...purposeful. It was an even bigger feeling than when I'd made it onto the force. I'd hesitated and waffled about becoming a police officer, unsure that was the right path to take if I wanted to help people. And now... Yeah, what I'd do with the Norlons would absolutely help people—two different sorts of people even. Sure, yes, there would be those who'd probably see me as some kind of traitor, but they were wrong. Even if there was some price to pay for what the Norlons could provide, it would be worth paying. I had no doubt about that. None.

Now that the call was over, the monitor was back to acting like a window. My quarters were somewhere on the interior of the Norlons' ship, but the display was letting me look at a view of Earth. I took a couple steps back and cocked my head, thinking we might be over some part of northern Russia at the moment. I'd been unconscious for the trip up here and this just didn't quite feel real. Maybe I could find an actual window that would drive home where I truly was.

I heard a ding-dong chime behind me and recognized it

from when Bashtine had come to Alam's quarters with all of the paperwork to make me official. I went over and saw live video of Kevin standing in the hall, so I touched the panel to open the door.

"Hey," I said, "whatcha got there?" I stepped back to let him.

"Clothes and other essentials." He carried a white box that he took over to set on the end of the bed. "I guessed that we're about the same size, but if anything doesn't fit, we can try again."

"Oh, cool. Thanks." I opened the box to take a look.

I'd asked to go down to the planet and pack, but Alam wasn't ready to return yet. Understandable, really, but it did leave me without a lot of stuff. I'd known Kevin would be along to help me out, but hadn't realized he'd deliver. "Is there somewhere that I can get essentials, like deodorant and toothpaste?"

"Oh, you bet. We'll go there after you change."

Since Kevin wore the same sort of robe-like tunic Alam had taken off, I wasn't surprised to see them in the box.

Actually, a few years back I'd gone to an Indian wedding as a then-boyfriend's plus one, and the groom had worn something a lot like these. The top I held up was a long-sleeved coat kind of deal in turquoise that would hang below my knees and had some frill to the bottom hem. The matching pants would be skintight. I was probably going to look pretty damn fancy in this stuff. Well, except for my combat boots.

"Any chance I can get some other shoes?" I asked Kevin. "All I have are my uniform boots." I pointed to where I'd left them by the door.

"I put some shoes in the bottom, but what size are you?"

I lifted out the clothes onto the table, and there were the slipper-like shoes. "I'm an eleven."

He smiled. "Me, too, so you're good to go."

"Wait, are these your clothes?"

"Yeah?"

"Aw, man, thanks. I really appreciate it. I'll get them back to you as soon as I can get my own stuff."

Kevin waved that away. "This is just to last you until you get measured so the tailors can make you a whole wardrobe. I think it'll take maybe six days, so you've got six sets of clothes in there. Oh, and we don't—"

I had to interrupt him. "A tailor and a wardrobe?"

"Well, as an official member of the delegation staff now," he said with a wink, "you'll need to dress the part. They gave you your police uniform, right? Same thing."

I was speechless for a second. These clothes weren't as bejeweled as that groom's wedding outfit had been, but they were still fancier than my uniform. "Yeah, okay. This being my new uniform makes sense. Um, what were you going to say?"

"Oh, just that underwear is not a Norlon concept," Kevin said with a chuckle, "so you can wash and wear whatever you've got, or you can go native."

I laughed at his little hip wiggle. "Alrighty then. When in Rome, I guess. But how do I wash everything?"

"Ah, right." He went to stand in the little bathroom, and I followed him, standing in the doorway since it wasn't big enough for both of us. "This receptacle here," he said, "delivers dirty clothes to the laundry and clean clothes back here. You'll put them in, push the button, and they get wrapped up and tagged specific to this room. They'll be back in the morning."

"Well, that's awesome. I hated doing laundry. Now, though, I'm wondering what time it is up here."

Kevin traded places with me while saying, "The ship is tuned to the Eastern US time zone since Prince Ye Lena wanted to land in Cleveland. We're also in what's called a stationary orbit above Canada, so our days and nights will match up, too. Both have made it easier to coordinate all the meetings everyone's had, so we'll be sticking to it."

"The Norlons are being really accommodating, you know?" Alone in the bathroom, I stripped out of my uniform, including my underwear, and put everything in the laundry receptacle. "They've really made things as easy as possible for everyone on Earth, even though they don't actually have to."

"Honestly, that's just how they are," Kevin said from the other room. "They have their vices and problems like anyone else, of course, but with this? Man, they're all in for making this about helping a new friend succeed."

"That just... Kevin, it makes me want to protect them even more," I said with conviction just before discovering that the pants had a pouch for my cock and balls. I got myself all tucked into it and realized that while it felt kind of obscene, I looked a bit like a Ken doll from the outside. Which explained why Alam's package had been more of a tease than a porn show.

Kevin chuckled. "I know. Same here. My wife's a Pip and thankfully, she loves how protective I am about her."

"Your wife's name is Pip?" I asked, not sure I'd heard

him right as I buttoned up my coat and came out of the bathroom.

"No, she's Norlon. Specifically, a Pip."

"No shit?" I'd known the Furries on Earth were all for fucking the Norlons, but not how the Norlons felt about that. If Kevin, a human, was married to a Norlon, then that was really good news. "Which one's are the Pips?" I had to ask since Alam hadn't mentioned them.

"Floria is a gray rabbit," he said with a grin and waggled his eyebrows.

I laughed with him. "Aw, man, that's good to hear. It feels like…permission, you know? I'm not wrong to feel some attraction."

"Hell, no, you're not wrong to be curious or up for it or anything else." He got me a pair of shoes from the box and dropped them in front of me. "And if someone catches your eye, know that Norlons love a direct approach, so don't be shy."

"Direct? Seriously?" I put the shoes on and felt like I was standing on a cloud. "Oh, damn, these are nice."

"You should absolutely ask if they're interested." He held out a hand. "Politely, of course. I got Floria by asking if she might like to get to know me more intimately."

In my mind, I replayed Alam saying he was intrigued by me. "Um, are there any sort of no fraternization rules for employees of the delegation?"

"No." Kevin frowned before his face brightened. "Oh, it's like that already, huh?"

I stood up a little straighter. "Yeah, it is."

CHAPTER 5
ALAM

Back in the large conference space on the ship, I was pleased to see that Kevin had escorted Logan here already. I was even more pleased to see that Logan wore traditional Norlon clothes in a blue that made his eyes seem to glow. When he smiled upon seeing me, I nearly lost my breath. He looked so very happy.

I smiled back and walked over to him, willing to adhere to his assertion that we remain colleagues without any physical intimacy. Though the urge to touch him was difficult to resist once I stood before him, I managed it.

"That color suits you well," I said.

"Thanks. Kevin loaned me a few outfits, but we stopped at the tailors on the way here. They scanned me everywhere," he said on a chuckle, "and I should have my own clothes in a few days."

I'd asked that they rush the job so that he wouldn't feel out of place or separate as he worked with us.

"You look great in gold," Logan said as a blush tinged his cheeks.

I ached to kiss him. Something about his new position must agree with him because he was more beautiful than before. I suddenly wanted to ensure that he never put on that dark and ill-fitting police uniform again.

"Come," I said, holding a hand out to guide him. "Let me introduce a few members of the delegation to you who might most benefit from your knowledge."

I led him toward the captain of the ship, Pysina Langarus, a Lago, who was talking with Rampon and other security personnel. While Logan's idea for a website had been readily taken on by members of the technology team, I knew security was where we needed Logan the most.

I made the introductions and then stood back and watched as Logan asked questions about the armor security personnel wore and the weapons they had. He was very open about offering what he knew of how human weapons could be used to defeat our protections.

At one point, Logan squinted at Rampon. "You don't have *any* projectile weapons? Nothing that shoots anything at all?"

Rampon held out his hand palm up and flexed his fingers, causing curved black talons to suddenly appear at his fingertips. "We *are* the weapon. You have no honor if you fight me any other way."

Logan's eyes widened as he stared at Rampon's retractable claws, and I could hear Logan gulp. "Right," he said, refocusing on the rest of us. "Well, um, you'll need to think of humans as a whole lot of folks without a lick of honor then. Especially in America, we're a lot more likely to shoot you from a distance than get up in your face. Not that we won't do that, too, though."

"*You* are not without honor," I had to interject. "When you saved my life, you were entirely honorable."

Logan softly smiled at me, and my heart seemed to flutter at the sight. "Okay," he said, "but it's better if you think of me as the exception, not the rule." His smile vanished as he said seriously, "Because we also have snipers who can shoot you from a mile away and intercontinental missiles."

I knew about those from talking to the humans on Nor, but now that we were in orbit above Earth, a chill went through me, and my fur stood up along my back. "Logan, could one of those missiles reach us here?"

"Oh. Uh… No? I can look into it, but I don't think anyone has that kind of capability." He shrugged as he looked between the rest of us. "Humans have been focused on shooting each other, and we know what it'll mean to do that. We have the ability to destroy ourselves and our planet, but I'm pretty sure none of our weapons can leave the atmosphere." He held out a hand to Pysina. "And, honestly, you'd see it coming with plenty of time to get out of the way or shoot back or…something. Right? Because we don't have anything like your space travel abilities, so anything we shot at you would come from the surface."

"Captain," I said as calmly as I could, "would you be so kind as to change our orbit?"

"Immediately, Your Highness." He gave me a brief bow before walking toward one of his aides near the doors. Moments later, the young Pip bolted from the room as the captain rejoined us. "We'll move into a higher orbit shortly."

"Sorry," Logan said with a wince.

"No, this is good." I rested my hand on his shoulder. "This is why we need you. While others have explained what they knew about human weaponry, they were farther removed from the source than you are and couldn't say what advancements humans might have made in the years since they were on Earth."

Logan shook his head, concentration on his face. "I'm no expert either, but I feel like our ability to destroy is about the same. We just aim better nowadays." He took a deep breath and sighed. "I'm not even sure anyone in authority would tell me the truth about what modern missiles could do."

Because he was fraternizing with us? It was a shame that we couldn't come to the humans and be accepted, trusted without proof of our intentions. They were a skittish people, but that made sense if they were forever concerned that another human would harm them and everyone they knew. Perhaps we could ease that stress for them someday.

"Anyway," Logan said, "back to where this started. If your armor can stop a small, high-velocity projectile like a bullet, then I think you'll be better protected for your next visit to the surface."

Rampon nodded, consulting his tablet. "I will confirm the velocity of your bullets and the strength of our armor and... Well, I'll let the scientists run some tests and get back to me."

"Excellent," I said, "thank you, everyone." To Logan, I said, "Allow me to introduce you to those working on the website now."

"Oh, great! I'm glad you were able to figure it out."

Logan walked with me toward another group of people huddled around a large screen with several pieces of information visible. When I saw the way Ghosha's gaze slid down Logan's body, I had an urge to loop an arm around Logan and stake my claim to him. No doubt the Khess was leading the sexual portion of the information-sharing, and I had to wonder how much Logan already knew, if anything.

Perhaps knowing more would help him change his mind about me?

"Oh, alright," Logan said before laughing uncomfortably. "You're going to need to put some kind of a warning on the pages where info about genitalia and sex is, um, going to be available."

"A warning?" a young Lago asked, peering up at Logan. "About what?"

"We have laws protecting minors—children—from sexual content." He held up a hand. "I'm not saying don't share it, just that you need some way of having the viewer agree that they're of the right age to see what's behind the warning. Um, it's like—"

"Wait," a Beku said excitedly, "I saw something about that. I know what that is."

Those Norlons creating the website huddled closer together, watching the Beku and making delighted noises as she made some sort of changes. Whatever they were using looked rather primitive, but they seemed quite enthusiastic about making it work for us.

"Hello," Ghosha said in his most seductive voice as he held a hand out to Logan. "I'm Ghosha Rijal."

Logan flicked a glance up at me, blushing, before giving

Ghosha his hand. "Logan Parrish. I'm, um, consulting with Alam."

"Alam is it?" Ghosha said with a grin for me.

I briefly bared my teeth at him, but Ghosha only laughed.

"Oh, I mean, Prince Ye Lena," Logan quickly amended. "Sorry."

"Don't worry," Ghosha said, enveloping Logan's hand. "If the prince has given you permission to be so familiar, I'm sure it's a gratifying situation for you both."

Why did everything the Khess said always sound so sexual? It was clear to me that Logan was aware of the implications as well when he peered up at me with an expression of apology or maybe worry.

I gave in to touching Logan and put an arm around his shoulders. That he edged a bit closer to me, let me know the contact was wanted. Ghosha caught the hint as well and grinned at me as he let Logan's hand go.

"Have you ever given any thought," Ghosha said to Logan, "to a career in sexual pleasure?"

Logan startled under my arm. "Excuse me?"

"Ghosha," I warned.

"Yes, Your Highness?" he said so innocently.

"Logan is here to consult on the best ways to integrate with the humans and—"

"Would that not include my goals?" Ghosha interrupted. "You did request that my team find the most acceptable methods of propositioning the humans."

I sighed. "Yes, I did."

"Uh," Logan said, "are Norlons looking for… Are you actually interested in, um…"

"Human sexual partners," Ghosha supplied with a leer. "Norlons and humans share a similar sexual appetite and have enjoyed discovering the many ways we are physically compatible with each other. My team's goal is to recruit as many humans as are willing to relocate to Nor and work in the brothels."

"Brothels," Logan said a bit breathlessly. "Wow. Okay."

"We are aware that it is a sensitive subject amongst some humans. I had asked Ghosha to find respectful methods of opening such discussions." I gestured to the screen and the text within a large orange star. "Must it ask so boldly for someone who enjoys sex to click here?"

Logan started snickering quietly, but it escalated to a full belly laugh that had him wiping tears from his eyes. I smiled at him, glad he wasn't offended at least, and waited for him to catch his breath.

"Woo! Okay," Logan finally managed to say. "Um, I think you should aim all of the marketing for your stuff at the Furries. They're the ones who've been—"

"The lovers," Ghosha purred.

Logan chuckled and nodded. "Yep, them. They're a ready-made population who won't have any problem with what you're proposing. I mean, not all of them might be into sex with Norlons, but they won't be upset about it." He cleared his throat and noticeably deflated. "Others won't be so cool with any of this. They're going to say some pretty horrible things. There might even be… I'm not sure, but they could get violent."

I hugged him against my side, moved by his concern for us. "We're aware of the potential." I looked Ghosha in the eyes. "Which is why we're going to be far more discreet going forward."

Ghosha had the grace to bow his head before asking the techs watching us to change the text inside the star to ask that Furries click there. "Let us also reexamine the language used to entice their applications," he added.

Logan smiled up at me, and again, I had a near overwhelming urge to lean down and kiss him. Perhaps that showed on my face or something else gave me away, because Logan blushed, and I could've sworn I read desire in his eyes.

If he was changing his mind about the parameters of our relationship, I would encourage him. But not here with Ghosha watching. I led Logan to another group of delegates, this one focused on medical advancements we were offering to the humans. We could revisit our relationship the next time we were alone.

CHAPTER 6

LOGAN

Days passed with me feeling more and more like I had a real purpose because every person I talked to actually valued my input. I didn't have to fight to prove my point or take a stand that someone else would stand against. Nobody doubled down or demanded to speak to my superior. The fact that everyone was counting on me, seeking me out, made me want to give them the best of everything I had.

I ended each day exhausted but I also couldn't stop smiling.

Tonight, I was having dinner with Alam in his quarters, and I wanted to let him know how much I was in love with my job. I wanted to thank him.

And yeah, maybe part of that would be me letting him know I also wanted to be more than professional colleagues. Not as my thank-you, but because I was getting to know him a lot more and liking the kind of person he was. Considerate, open to new ideas, supportive, and willing to admit when he didn't know something and needed help—those were all qualities I hadn't even realized I found attractive until Alam. He was an excellent leader, and I was learning a lot from him.

The ember of want I'd been fanning for him had grown into a bonfire. I couldn't resist anymore.

My new wardrobe had been delivered a couple days ago, so I'd given Kevin back all of his outfits and shoes and was really enjoying mine. The tailors deserved raises because the colors they'd chosen for me were perfect. I was turning heads all over the ship, which was happening now as I made my way to Alam's quarters. I'd changed from the deep red I'd worn all day to cream with all kinds of sparkles across the chest. I'd been propositioned by a Pip once already, but my sights were set on Alam.

The end of the hall on Alam's floor was guarded, which meant he knew I was coming because he had to approve my entrance. That he was standing in his doorway before I got there had me thinking he was looking forward to seeing me outside of work, too.

"Ah, Logan." His voice was huskier than usual as his gaze tracked down my body.

I wasn't sure how to read his expression. "Yes?"

He grinned. "You look…very good in this color."

It was on the tip of my tongue to make a quip about looking better out of it, but I wanted to keep things classy with him. To start anyway. If he was a dirty-talking beast in bed, I'd put my ass in the air and beg.

"Thank you," I said politely and walked in when he stepped back.

"Would you like a drink while we decide on dinner options?"

"Sure, thanks. Something sweet and bold like last time?" Because being in here again was reminding me of the first time, when I'd stupidly told him no.

"It's an ale my family brews that's called fedesmia," he said from the bar near the sitting area where he was getting glasses. "Absolutely no one can say that correctly after three of them."

I laughed and accepted my drink before sitting down opposite him. "Good to know." I took a sip. "Mmm, yeah." It was a strong liquor, like whisky but somehow sweeter. I didn't want to get drunk, so I took another sip and set the glass down.

Watching Alam take a drink, I marveled at his black lips pursing and the way his long, pink tongue peeked out as he licked them. Despite having a snout, I knew he could kiss and a shiver of want went through me as I gave in to imagining that.

Alam's nostrils flared as he took a deep breath, and I realized half of what I wanted to say probably wouldn't need to be said. The rest, though, did.

"I wanted to thank you," I started, "for hiring me and letting me be a part of all this. It's honestly been the best experience of my life."

"Logan," he said, touching his chest. "I'm so pleased to hear that."

"As a cop, I thought I was doing something, but now? I really *feel* it. I'm helping. I'm making a difference."

"Oh, yes!" Alam set his glass on the table and reached over to rest his hand on my knee. "You are contributing in ways that are making a significant difference to our mission. Have they told you about the success of the website?" He grinned and squeezed my knee before sitting back.

"No, I was going to check in there tomorrow."

"I can tell you that there have been millions of views which have led to a noticeable change in media representation *and* public perception." He chuckled and shook his head. "Ghosha is thrilled by the seven thousand applicants."

I laughed, too, since I'd be one of them if I wasn't sitting here already. I cleared my throat, taking the shot since he'd set it up so well. "Um, Alam?"

"Hmm?"

"Someone told me that a direct approach was best with Norlons, so…" I couldn't help clearing my throat again. "I was wondering if maybe you'd like to change the, um, type of relationship we—"

"Yes."

I chuckled in relief at his quick answer and nodded.

"Would you allow me to mate you, Logan?"

I might not know exactly what sex with a Norlon was like, but the phrase "mate you" had me thinking I knew what one part would include.

"Yeah," I answered honestly. "I'd, um, like to do that." I gulped, as if that would help with how breathless I sounded.

Alam's smile was full of sharp teeth and lust, and I shivered. "Let me see you," he rumbled.

I stood up, praying he'd be that dominant the whole time, and he gave me his complete attention. I didn't want to think of Alam as a predator, but… Well, maybe I did? Because his piercing blue gaze seemed to catalog my every movement, and that sent a thrill through me, especially when I started opening my tunic.

I watched Alam grip the arms of his chair, sharp claws appearing and biting into the fabric. I bit my bottom lip as I imagined that he was restraining himself. He wanted to pounce and take me, but he held back, waiting, maybe even savoring the anticipation. So I made a show of getting my tunic off and flexing as I let it fall from my arms. The way he watched me was actually easing my nerves because his hunger never wavered. I *felt* how much Alam wanted me.

My cock was filling, throbbing, as I pulled the skin-tight pants away from my waist. Alam was taking deep breaths, and I realized he was inhaling the scent of my arousal. When he licked his lips in a way that The Big Bad Wolf would've admired, I grinned with the confidence of knowing that his hunger for me was growing.

Watching his every whisker twitch, I pushed my pants down to my thighs. Suddenly, Alam growled and lunged toward me. I stood straight with a gasp, and he clasped me to him with both strong arms. He didn't hesitate to lift me right off my feet and carry me across the room. In seconds, I was on his bed, and he was hauling his tunic over his head, not bothering with the buttons at all.

"You're a terrible tease," he said, his voice lower, rumbling as he came close to loom over me.

"I was hoping you'd pounce." I laughed a little breathlessly, my fingers delving deep into the thick black fur on his chest. "My god, you're so soft."

He grinned and pressed closer, making my arms go around him as his chest met mine. I moaned at the way his fur teased my bare skin. The enormous cock he still hid inside his formfitting pants ground down against mine. "Not all of me is soft."

"True. So true." I nodded, fingers petting his back. I'd never minded a hairy partner, but a furry one might just be ruining me for anyone else.

Alam's tongue snuck out and licked over my lips before he leaned away, reaching for my foot. He quickly had one shoe off and then the other before he eased my pants down and off my legs. I spread myself wide open, wanting him to look, begging him to touch.

After that lick, I should've known he'd use his tongue, but it was still a delicious surprise. With his cold, wet nose pressed into my lower belly, Alam lapped at my dick and balls like he was feasting on me. I didn't resist spreading my legs wider and couldn't have stopped myself from gripping the furry, black ruff at his neck to keep him there. He made obscene slurping noises and delighted hums as he licked and licked.

When he suddenly swallowed my whole cock to the root, I hollered in sharp pleasure. I also stared, amazed, since his snout was long enough that I probably wasn't even in his throat. Trembling hard as he started sucking, I kept whining from the brilliant sensation and knowing just how dangerous his teeth were.

His guttural growl made me yell wordlessly before I had to warn him. "Christ, Alam, you're going to make me come."

He pulled off with a smirk and stood up, reaching for his waistband. I sat up on my elbows, my aching cock mostly forgotten because I absolutely needed to see his.

That it was a bright pink surprised me, but that it was long and thick with a tapered head and a bulge halfway down had me pulling my legs back on pure wanton instinct.

"Do you want me to mate you, Logan?" Alam asked as he stroked himself. "Shall I fill your body and make you mine?" Precome beaded on the foreign head of his cock, and I licked my lips as I nodded.

"Yeah," I said, my voice sounding hoarse to my own ears. "Fuck, yeah."

He patted my thigh. "Turn over."

Doggy style. Dear god, it was so hard not to giggle at that even as I eagerly rolled onto my hands and knees. I didn't want to be the one to tell him the name we humans had given the position if no one had before me, but wow, it was both funny and sexy as hell.

I went down onto my elbows and tipped my ass up, my feet hanging over the edge of the bed as he walked to a bedside table. I was trying to take deep breaths to keep from panting already while I watched him pump lube into his hand and slick up his pink dick.

When he came back, I opened my mouth to tell him I needed some prep, but then all I did was gasp as his tongue was back on me. I grunted and pressed my face into the soft bedsheets while he was back there licking me open with his incredible tongue. It felt fantastic and I couldn't stop moaning from the dexterity and length of the thing. Like, he wasn't just licking around my rim, he was breaching it and stuffing his tongue inside me.

Prince Alam Ye Lena was fucking ruining me for anyone else. I really hadn't considered that he'd become my gold standard for the rest of my life. He hadn't even fucked me and I was already fucked.

Didn't stop me from begging for it, though. "Alam. Alam! Fuck me. Come on, *please*."

He withdrew his tongue and a slick finger eased inside my wet ass. I moaned at the intrusion, anticipation skittering through me. I heard him hum with delight when I started rocking back on his finger, taking it deeper each time. Then there were two stretching me and Alam growled, "You have a beautiful ass, Logan. My cock will look so good buried inside you."

"Oh, please," I begged as his fingers left me empty. "Alam, *please*."

His chuckle sounded dangerous just before I felt the wet tip of his cockhead touch my hole. I pushed back to receive him, and he rocked himself into me. I was panting as the head breached me and some kind of ridge right behind it made me open up again to let him in more. I buried my face in the bedding and moaned as he thrust in and out, going steadily deeper. He was big and thick and perfect.

I actually whimpered when he lay over my back, his arms long enough to bracket me and claws out again to poke into the bedding. His furry body rubbed against me from shoulders to ass, the soft warmth contrasting with the pure, solid strength of him. And then he lowered his head, snarling teeth right there beside my face, and I shivered so hard I nearly came.

"Logan, goddess…" he said like it was torn out of him, and I loved that he was as caught up in the pleasure as I was.

"I'm come— Ugh! Coming!"

He fucked me through it as my whole body spasmed and my untouched cock shot all over the bed. But then I felt him push deeper, like maybe he hadn't been giving me his whole cock until then. I wailed in sharp pleasure as a bulbous part of his amazing cock made my hole stretch wider to let him in. Then Alam was coming, growling and barking, one arm looped under me and up to my shoulder, claws threatening to pierce my skin.

Alam twitched and panted against me, while I gasped for breath and swam in the bliss of a fantastic fuck. I was seriously wrecked. No one would ever be able to do me as good as Alam just had.

"Logan," he said between panting breaths, "I knotted you."

"What?"

He relaxed his hold on me, but didn't pull away. "I didn't mean to, but I gave you my knot. We're bound together until it relaxes."

I felt my eyes widen as I remembered hearing about that. It happened with dogs—probably all of the canines actually. And now with us. Alam's cock was literally stuck in my ass and locking us together.

Laughter snuck up on me and I was quickly breathless all over again.

"Well, at least you're not upset," Alam muttered as he maneuvered us higher onto the bed while holding me to him, and then tipped us over and spooned me.

My laughter faded to a happy sigh since I was tucked close against him and wrapped in his furry warmth. I hugged his arms around me and liked that he could rest his chin on top of my head.

As sleep tugged at me, I mumbled, "You're never getting rid of me now."

CHAPTER 7
ALAM

Logan's whispered words pierced straight to my heart. Did he mean them? Would he stay with me? Or was that just the bliss of our sex talking for him? I felt Logan's breathing even out as sleep claimed him and cradled him in my arms.

I'd never knotted someone. Normally, I did take the more dominant role, but I had not lost my senses to the point of forcing my knot into a partner. I should have asked Logan if he would want to take it, but I hadn't thought I might act on such an instinct. That he hadn't minded the intrusion and now trusted me enough to sleep in my arms had me wondering if that was why I'd done it. Could I have known Logan was the one to knot?

I took a deep breath, savoring the scent of our mating. From the first, Logan had smelled like something special, but the circumstances of our meeting hadn't allowed me to explore what his aroma might mean. Thinking about it now, I had to wonder if when my people whispered about scenting their mate, they meant exactly that: their fragrance was something one recognized with one's whole heart.

My knot was shrinking, allowing our bodies to separate, but I didn't want to leave him. I wanted to start again, fill him a second time, bind us together once more. That he was asleep kept me from doing so, of course, but the idea of waking him up with an orgasm was an intriguing idea as well.

In a moment, our bodies took care of separating us, and I sighed and scooted back. I gently massaged his hole, encouraging it to relax, and Logan moaned as he pushed back against me. Smiling, I kissed his cheek before standing to get us properly cleaned. I'd filled him so full, some of my essence was leaking back out of him, so I used a damp cloth made for such things to wipe him off. Logan moaned and pulled one leg up, making me chuckle for how he wanted me even in sleep. Had he been awake, I would have bathed him with my tongue.

Twice now, I'd been tempted to lick him clean. I would have to see that I did it at some point or the longing and denial would drive me mad.

I cleaned myself off, my cock hanging heavily, unsheathed and ready for another round. I was not normally so eager, so wired, after mating a partner. I should be luxuriating in the bliss of completion at the very least, but I couldn't relax for wanting him again.

"Mmm, Alam…" Logan mumbled as he curled his fingers around his cock.

"I'm here," I whispered and loomed over him, eager to watch if he meant to pleasure himself.

He blinked sleepy eyes up at me and smiled. "Should've

probably said I always conk out after really good sex." He stopped touching himself and ran his fingers through the fur on my chest, moaning quietly.

My cock stiffened and I lowered my hips to rub against him. "If you sleeping proves our sex was really good, then I will take it as the compliment it is."

Logan chuckled, nodding, before he bit his bottom lip and his fingers tugged at my fur as he thrust up against me in return. His lips parted, breath beginning to pant, and a flush pinked his cheeks as he stared up at me with low-lidded eyes. Logan was the personification of desire, and I was powerless to resist.

I kneed his legs farther apart and reached down to grip one asscheek as I ground harder against him. He made the sweetest whimper, our cocks sliding along each other and sacs bumping. Logan hooked his ankles behind me, locking us together as securely as my knot had done.

But then he stopped moving. "Wait," he said.

I stilled with worry. "What's wrong?"

"Nothing. I just…" He gulped and took a deep breath like he was trying to calm himself. "I like this—it's so good feeling you on top of me—but I want… If you wouldn't mind—"

"There is very little I wouldn't allow you, Logan." I licked his upper lip briefly and smiled. "Ask me."

"Can I taste you?"

As if I would deny him that. "Yes, of course." I pushed up to stand over him. "How would you like me?"

His gaze roamed over me from head to cock and he seemed to lose his words for a few moments. "Uh… Sitting. In the chair?"

I did as instructed and went to sit in the chair I'd occupied earlier. That he wanted to kneel at my feet and fill his mouth with my cock was a fantasy I'd indulged in just last evening. To have him walk over, hard cock swaying, and get on his knees between my legs was a dream come true.

"Goddess, Logan," I said, my voice a rumble. "You look divine just there."

He gave me a grin and slid his hands through the fur on my thighs, the contrast between us adding to my arousal. My cock bobbed, drawing his attention, and he leaned in to gently lick the head. I couldn't help the way my breath stuttered at the sight and feel of him, and then I moaned throatily as he sucked just the tip into his warm, wet mouth.

My claws came out and I dug them into the arms of the chair as I watched Logan explore my cock with his lips and tongue. He was curious and thorough, mapping the veins and ridges, and then sucking on the bulge of my knot. I groaned at the ceiling as my hips bucked without permission.

"I wonder if I can take you again," he whispered.

I forced the words out even though instinct had me wanting to flip him around and take him. "Be certain," I growled, claws gouging deeper into the chair.

Logan grinned as he stood up and walked over to get a palmful of lubricant from beside the bed. Knowing he meant to let me back into his tight, hot body sent a shiver of ferocious desire through me. And then he was coating my cock in slick and licking his lips as I snarled from the pleasure of his firm touch. I didn't dare release the arms of the chair as he climbed onto my lap, facing me. Kneeling high, he aimed my cock at his hole and slowly sank down, bringing us back together.

With my cock buried in him to the flare of my knot, Logan grinned at me. "Knot me again?"

My breath caught. "Are you certain?"

He nodded. "Oh, yeah. That felt amazing." He smirked and petted the ruff at my neck. "And if I need any help later, there's always the nanobots."

That he was willing to risk injury—even one that could be easily healed—both pleased and frightened me because I could not resist him. What Logan wanted, I would give him.

Of course, that he wanted a slow mating of him rising and falling on my cock with a maddening pace sorely tested my patience and restraint for an achingly long time. I matched his rhythm, thrusting up as he sank down, and watched how his face flushed and breaths panted through kiss-swollen lips. Every little gasp and moan out of him was mine and instinct drove me to give him what he'd asked for without hesitation.

I grabbed his hips and pushed him down at the same time as I drove my cock up. The sudden move had my knot punching into him, stretching him open and locking us together. Logan threw his head back and hollered, his cock erupting between us as his ass spasmed along my full length. I crushed him against me and followed him over, filling his body and claiming him as my own yet again.

As Logan lay heavily against my chest, I wrapped my arms around him and knew I would never be able to let him go.

Logan and I spent our days seeing to our work and our nights together in my quarters. Halaby had provided Logan with a salve to use after I knotted him that would help him recover faster. I'd endured knowing grins from the doctor since we were both aware that it was a salve normally reserved for newly joined mates locked in the frenzy to claim each other. I felt that being able to do my duties without Logan perched on my cock meant we were not in a frenzy at all. Halaby disagreed.

So did Ghosha. He also thought it was all terribly romantic. That he chose to discuss it with me while we were on the transport down to Earth had me twitching in my seat. At least he spoke in Norlish so Logan couldn't understand him.

"Hush, Ghosha," I said for the hundredth time.

"Why? Clearly, you need someone to point out the obvious to you." He patted my thigh. "Worry not, I'm certain you won't be the only one of us to find a human mate. They are rather irresistible." He grinned in Logan's direction. "Look how he cannot resist checking on you and blushing as he does."

We were seated several rows apart as befitted our different ranks, but Ghosha wasn't wrong that Logan kept glancing my way and blushing when our eyes met. No doubt every Norlon in this confined space knew from the scents of us how we both longed to be alone again.

But that did not mean he was my destined life mate.

"We have discussed nothing about our relationship," I

said quietly to Ghosha. "I should like to speak with *him* before I confirm anything with *you*."

Ghosha grunted and wiggled in his seat. "Your denial speaks volumes, my friend."

I sighed and ignored the annoying Khess for the rest of the flight.

Yesterday, the armor that Logan had helped Rampon design had finally been ready for us all. I'd had little reason to delay a return to the surface of Earth after that. Though we had accomplished much during our absence, all agreed that being seen was still important to the success of our mission. Especially now that we knew how much better the humans were responding to direct information rather than what was filtered through their representatives.

I wasn't eager to set foot on the planet again, but it felt necessary. I comforted myself by remembering that I wouldn't have met Logan if I hadn't done this before. And we could gauge how the humans accepted us much better now, so we knew more of them were interested in partnering with us for various reasons. Visiting again was the right thing to do.

The Humans First organization was still a concern, but I felt we were all far more prepared to meet the threat than before. Security would be on high alert, were all armed with offensive and defensive weaponry, and none of them would defer to human security personnel. Yes, the human authorities would not be pleased by any of that, but I refused to allow us to be caught at a disadvantage just to make them feel more secure. Maybe they needed to know that we had the means to go to war but chose not to? If that made them see us as strong and capable rather than weak and vulnerable, then so be it.

When the shuttle touched down, Logan was immediately by my side. "I had an idea," he said, his cheeks flushed pink and eyes shining.

"What is your idea?" I stood up and patted the armor under my clothes to make it lay flat again. It was made of several small, overlapping panels that seemed to have a tendency to crinkle in upon each other. Thankfully, I had seen it stop a high-speed projectile, so I didn't mind the occasional pinch to my fur.

"Last time, the human leaders hustled you all past the reporters, right?" Logan fell into step with me as we moved toward the exit. "I think it would be better if you all stopped and talked to them. Let them get their answers directly from Norlons, you know?"

"Instead of filtered through the human authorities." I rested my hand at the base of his neck and gave him an appreciative massage. "Excellent thinking."

I paused at the exit and turned to the rest of the delegation behind us. "We will be speaking to the reporters this time. You know your messages, and I have every confidence in your abilities to educate and reassure the humans. Should you need assistance, seek it out."

I waited to see the majority of them talking to their staff or referencing their tablets before continuing toward the exit. "Did you hear?" I asked Rampon as I approached him.

Only when Rampon glanced at Logan did I realize I still held him. I patted Logan and let him go, clearing my throat in embarrassment.

Rampon nodded at me. "Yes, Your Highness. We will support that going in and coming back out, if you wish."

"Ah, yes," I said, looking at Logan, "then we can explain what we wish to accomplish as well as the outcome."

"Perfect." Logan smiled up at me and briefly touched the back of my hand.

I had to look away from him and focus on what we were about to do or else I might ravish him where he stood.

As we departed the shuttle and the crowds of humans sent up a deafening cheer, I couldn't help admitting that my attraction to Logan was incredibly strong. But mates? I had no experience there and it would be quite complicated given my rank. I was meant to mate for alliance or breeding. Mating Logan would do none of that. I was certain—as was my mother—that her mating to Carl had been approved only because she had already done her duty by having me and my siblings with our father.

Logan would be my first mate.

I glanced at him and couldn't help thinking that I wanted him to be my last as well. The heavy thump of my heart then made me a little more aware that he did mean something to me. But was it lust, or love?

"Ready?" Logan asked over the noise of the crowd.

I nodded and opened my mouth to confirm it only to realize I didn't know what he was asking me. Ready to make him my mate? But no, when he glanced toward the exit, I knew he meant was I ready to speak to the human reporters.

I cleared my throat and put a hand over my pounding heart. "Yes, I'm ready."

We walked down the ramp and out into the open, Rampon and his guards taking their positions all around us. President Conway, a rather round human man who led the country of America, approached me with a big smile on his face. "Welcome back, Your, uh, Highness."

Why did he address me like that every time? Even in our video conferences, he always inserted that hesitation. I was beginning to think he might doubt my royalty.

"Thank you," I said and didn't bother to use his title at all.

"If you'll just come this way," he said and gestured to a different entrance than before. "We'll get you inside faster this time around."

I had no idea why he winked. Thankfully, once the meetings began, he often left the discussions up to his staff and other members of his government. Some of the other world leaders were far more capable, but those like Conway seemed only interested in having their photographs taken with us.

"While I appreciate that," I told him and gestured in the opposite direction, "we would like to speak with the reporters first."

I turned and began walking toward them, smiling as they clearly grew excited at the prospect of our approach. Some of them already started yelling questions at us.

"Uh, no, I don't believe that's on the agenda," Conway blustered as he hustled to keep up with me. "We're on a bit of a time crunch, you see, and—"

I ignored him and kept going with the rest of the delegation, our guards fanning out as we approached. Now that Logan had planted the seed of how we Norlons should and could control more of our own messaging, I was eager to disallow anyone else to do it.

The reporters were contained behind a barrier and were all leaning forward with various devices held out toward us. I flattened my ears back to protect my hearing as they shouted over top of each other. When they surged forward, I put up my hands and waved them back, fearing they might crush each other or trample the human security personnel holding up the barriers.

"Be easy," I told hollered over them. "I will answer your questions. Please be careful with each other."

It seemed to throw them off that the entire delegation was in front of them, spread out with their staff members and guards, because there was a brief moment of silence.

But only briefly.

"Officer Parrish! Is it true that you resigned from the police force to work for the aliens?"

"Yes, it's true that I work for *the Norlons* now," Logan said with a pointed stare. "Prince Ye Lena offered me a consulting position with the delegation, and I accepted."

I liked his emphasis on our name, and then I felt his fingers brushing mine. Hidden by the folds of my clothing and his, I caught his hand and held on, offering and gaining comfort.

"And your injuries?" another reporter asked. "We were told they were mild and—"

"Well, no, they weren't *mild*. I had severe bruising on my back and a badly broken nose, but I healed quickly thanks to Doctor Revazi's nanobots."

Again, there was a brief silence before a flurry of questions. It seemed that though they were aware of the medical advancements we wished to share, they may not have believed we truly had the capabilities we'd explained on the new website. Logan was doing his best, but when he directed them to Halaby again, I stepped in.

"Truly, if you wish the most accurate explanation of any medical procedure or device we are offering, you should speak with members of the medical team." I smiled and gestured down the row to Halaby.

A few of the reporters broke off and moved down the line, and I was glad for it. I wanted them to get the most factual information and, though I could speak to the wonders of the nanobots with awe, I couldn't necessarily explain how they functioned with any degree of accuracy.

"What do you say to those accusing the Norlons of sex trafficking?"

That gave me pause and I focused on the reporter who'd spoken. "I don't understand that phrase, but your use of the word 'accusing' worries me. Could you expand please?"

"Oh, um…" She wet her lips nervously and glanced around. "Well, sex trafficking is forcing people to perform sex acts as a form of slave—"

"Goddess, no!" I hollered, startled that such a heinous crime could be associated with us. "We have no desire whatsoever to *force* anyone to do anything." I knew I should direct them to Ghosha, but it seemed imperative that I address this immediately. "On Nor, sex work is legal and a legitimate profession. It is not a career suited for everyone, of course, but those who choose it are provided excellent wages, housing, and medical care. We seek human sex workers willing to relocate and join our thriving sex industry simply because there are so few of them on Nor and interest is high. We do understand that many human authorities disallow sex work on Earth, but were it legal and supported here, Norlons would happily relocate as well. In fact, an exchange of sex workers would be the ideal situation."

The reporter blinked up at me with her lips slightly parted. Since she said nothing more, I nodded to her and looked to the next person.

It went on like that for some time until the questions died down. I chuckled since that seemed to surprise them as well. Several wished us luck with the negotiations, and I assured them we would return for more questions before leaving. By their slack-jawed responses, it was clear their own people didn't afford them such transparency.

As I walked toward the entrance Conway had indicated earlier, I realized I still held Logan's hand. I wasn't sure if anyone else had noticed, but his smile as he looked up at me lit something in my heart that I wanted to keep.

CHAPTER 8
LOGAN

Sitting along the wall with the rest of the support staff, I listened to the big wigs on both sides negotiate. Well, I wanted to call it negotiate, but it was a lot of negative responses from the humans every time the Norlons tried again. My fellow humans had me feeling like I was watching a presidential debate—the kind where they made a lot of promises and insisted that they had all the answers, but never actually said anything. And they were the ones being offered solutions! Alam and the rest were handing over whatever we could need to improve our lives, and these world leaders were saying variations of the phrase "I'll think about it and get back to you."

I could understand that some of it was overwhelming and maybe they didn't trust how great the Norlons insisted some thing was. So, fine, they could test the thing until they felt better about it. I really could understand that and even support that way of thinking. But it was starting to sound like the human politicians weren't interested in testing or trying. It felt like they were refusing, but wanting to sound like there was still a chance, stringing the Norlons along.

Like with the nanobots. Doctor Revazi was willing to hand over not just vats of the things, but the knowledge and tech necessary to make the microscopic robots. I was pretty sure we humans didn't have anything of the sort, so why wouldn't my leaders embrace the opportunity? But they weren't! These fat cats were nodding their heads and making noises like they were fascinated, but not one of them said anything close to wanting the nanobots, research, or technology.

Bet if there had been a single human scientist in the room right now, they would've been weeping. Hell, I wanted to cry from watching these people operate because Revazi just said curing certain types of cancer might be possible. And the humans were blustering about testing, distribution, insurance, jobs…

"Then we'll start our own company," I muttered, arms crossed and slumping in my chair, hating every second of this bullshit.

"A company?" the Norlon sitting beside me said. I was getting better about remembering the types, and I thought she was a Lago since she looked like a fox.

"I'm just seriously getting frustrated with all this," I said by way of apology for distracting her.

"No, no. Tell me what you mean." She looked open and eager. After hours of listening to my people say no, I couldn't resist telling her everything on my mind.

"Well, okay." I sat up and kept my voice low. "If the governments don't want to distribute whatever it is the Norlons are offering, then the Norlons should do it themselves. Start companies—like a company that distributes nanobots. People can go online and fill out a form stating what's wrong with them, include—I don't know—a note from their doctor or something, and they get a vial of the right kind of nanobots. Or maybe it's a pill or a shot of juice—whatever. And maybe the company isn't even selling medical stuff since that's probably super regulated, but we call it a supplement or a food product. We adhere to whatever guidelines or laws exist for selling that kind of thing even though we're not even selling it, and ta-da, people don't need to wait for their politicians to do something because they can go right around them and do it themselves."

I ran out of steam and sat back with a shrug. She was beaming at me as she turned her tablet around so I could see the screen. Everything I'd said was written out in English.

"Is this accurate?" she asked me.

"Uh, yeah. Why did you record all that?"

"So that I can send it to the delegation."

She tapped a button, and I looked over at the table to see every Norlon tablet light up with the message. My heart nearly stopped. Yeah, sure, that was the sort of thing they were paying me to do, but here? Now?

In a moment, the tablets belonging to those of us lining the walls started lighting up. The Lago next to me grinned as she let me see that Revazi was thrilled and wanting to find out what starting a nanobot company required. Before I could say something to her, my own tablet started blowing up with praise from the members of the delegation.

I felt my face heating as I blushed while reading their excited messages. They loved the idea of skirting around these authorities who didn't seem to be listening and going straight to the people they could help. They would eliminate this room full of middlemen and get right to the consumers who wanted the products—who maybe even needed them to survive.

Another message popped up on my tablet, this one from Alam.

> I'm going to ravish you the moment we're alone, you utterly brilliant man.

I cleared my throat to cover my laugh and looked up at Alam sitting in front of me. His back was to me, and his tail was wagging. *Wagging.* It was cute and flattering at the same time.

> I look forward to it, Your Highness.

His tail wagged faster.

"Let us table this conversation for now," Alam said loudly, "and turn our attention to the discussion of sex workers."

I didn't feel like that topic was going to go over any better, but did like the way half the humans in the room started fidgeting and turning red. Some blustering noises and coughs sounded from the other side of the table as Ghosha stood up.

I couldn't help wiggling a bit in my seat, a little giddy to watch the fireworks, but then there were three Norlons coming up to me. They had questions about the regulations they'd found relating to starting businesses and wanted to see if I could help them understand. Though I had a feeling a lot of it could end up being stuff I wouldn't get either, duty called. I got up and followed them over to a corner.

On the way, I gave Alam's tail a little tug just because I could.

THE NORLONS HAD SIX BUSINESS LICENSES BY THE TIME WE were on the shuttle back up to the ship. Everything was above board, totally legal, and they even had human lawyers helping them. I couldn't decide if I felt like a super villain or a hero—maybe both?—since working the system was sure to cause a rift between the delegation and all those global heads of state.

Honestly, I could see the point of some of my fellow humans' worries and all that—trust was hard sometimes—but I couldn't stand their lack of action. It probably had a lot to do with the type of people in charge. They'd never had to ask for help, to give up their pride and reach for someone else to show them the way out of a bad situation. And they didn't think of themselves as the helpers either, the one to do that for someone else. But me? Man, if there was a solution on the table, I was going to make every effort to grab it, make it, do it, or die trying.

And yeah, maybe some industries would suffer. But was anyone really going to feel bad for Big Pharma if they didn't have a trillion-dollar year? I sure wouldn't.

I was scrolling through my tablet and marveling at what the Norlons had accomplished so quickly as I trailed after Alam's entourage through the ship. Which was why I immediately saw the photo someone sent me of Alam and I holding hands. Their message said it was all over the news channels on Earth.

We'd walked the line of reporters again after the meeting and yeah, I'd been unable to resist letting Alam hold my hand when I felt the soft pads of his fingers brushing mine. He'd been so excited to tell the reporters what had been accomplished during the meeting—even if it hadn't been because the politicians had listened to us—and I'd gotten caught up in wanting to share in that excitement. Now a subsection of the news was all about our relationship.

And I didn't even know whether I could call it a relationship.

Suddenly, someone grabbed the front of my tunic and yanked me forward. I squawked and nearly dropped my tablet, looking up to find that it was Alam and we were in his quarters. Before I had a chance to wonder what had happened to everyone else, Alam got down to the ravishing he'd promised and kissed me like he was trying to steal my soul.

I kissed him back until I heard cloth rip and pulled my mouth free of his. "Don't you tear this," I said, batting at his claws. "It's my favorite outfit."

Alam snarled, baring his teeth, but took a step back. "You need to be naked, Logan."

I shivered at the growl in his voice and set my tablet

down. Grinning, I took my time getting out of my clothes properly.

He ripped his entire outfit clean off. Like literally snatched it all right off of his body with three swipes of his clawed hands. My cock took notice of that display of brute strength, perking up in the confines of my stretchy pants as I stood there staring. Alam was scenting the air, and I grinned to know that he could smell how much I wanted him. I kicked off my shoes and opened my jacket one button at a time.

Alam's cock was bright pink and leaking, the knot already looking like a challenge—one I couldn't resist taking, of course. His balls were high and tight, seeming desperate to flood me, and I licked my lips in anticipation.

In the time it took for my jacket to slide down my arms, Alam was suddenly in front of me and grabbing me, turning me around. My jacket hit the floor as I tripped over my own feet, and Alam pressed me down against the mattress with my ass in the air. I chuckled at his impatience and tried to work my pants down only to feel him grab the seat of them. I felt him rip my pants open, right down the seam, baring my ass to him.

Before I could protest how he'd just destroyed my favorite pants, I felt the pinprick of his claws as he held my cheeks apart and then the wet swipe of his tongue as he licked over my hole. I moaned into the bedding and locked my knees as he bathed my crack over and over. The threat of his teeth added to the delicious sensation of his tongue worming its way inside me, demanding I open for him. I wanted to do everything I could to obey him right then.

Satisfied or impatient, he stopped licking me, and I felt

the tapered head of his cock pressing for entrance. I let him in, the both of us slick and ready, and moaned as he steadily rocked himself deeper. When I felt the knot threatening, I lifted up on my toes and said, "Do it. Alam, knot me!"

He did. Fucking hell, it was torture and pure bliss at the same time as he forced my ass to open wide for his knot. I grunted and moaned with relief and a little pride as he popped inside of me and locked us together. Reaching down to fist my cock, wondering if I could get myself off and take him with me, I gasped as he wrapped his arms around me and lifted.

With me perched on his cock, Alam held me against his chest and walked over to sit in one of the chairs. I couldn't do anything but hold onto his arms in shocked amazement. He settled me on his lap and the pressure inside me had me throwing my head back and groaning at the ceiling. I might not need to stroke myself to get off. I was so close just like this.

"I cannot resist you," he rumbled in my ear, tongue snaking out to lick my cheek. His hands wandered, the velvety pads of his fingertips feeling so sweet against my inner thighs as his claws threatened. "Do you know how hard it was for me to keep my hands to myself today?"

"So hard," I said breathlessly before he pulled a whine out of me by using the heel of his hand to press my cock against my abs and rub on me. "Alam," I moaned when he cupped my sac, the prick of his claws making me shiver as he kept rubbing.

"So hard," he echoed. "I wanted to claim you on the

conference room table. Show everyone this brilliant, compassionate man is *mine*."

I nodded, unable to speak as his other hand pinched my nipple repeatedly, sending shockwaves of pleasure shooting through me. I couldn't think, wasn't sure, but I had a feeling that if Alam had asked to fuck me in that room full of pompous politicians, I'd have let him. God, I wanted to be claimed by him, belong to him. I forced myself to yell, "Alam, please!"

He rubbed just right against the head of my cock and growled, baring his teeth beside my head, and that was it for me. I hollered wordlessly and strained, arching my back and curling my toes, coming with that knot of his stuffing me so full. He locked an arm around my chest, his hips thrusting up, and I moaned to know he'd come, too.

Basking in the bliss coursing through me, I found myself rubbing my come-slicked belly and swearing I could feel the heat of his come locked inside me. I couldn't stop the happy little noises I made because I loved knowing Alam's knot was letting me absorb it, keep him with me. He was mine just as much as I was his.

CHAPTER 9

ALAM

Sweet Logan was asleep when my knot relaxed enough to lift him into my arms and carry him to bed. That urge to lick him clean was too strong to resist, but I only licked his shoulder every now and then as I spooned behind him. The warm scent of his sated body and our combined sex was the best thing I had ever smelled in my life.

"That tongue's gonna get you in trouble," Logan mumbled before he chuckled.

Since he wasn't upset, I confessed. "I've wanted to bathe you with it since the infirmary."

"Really?"

He turned, trying to see me, and I released him so he could roll onto his back. I sat up on my elbow and nodded, eyeing him warily since I knew humans didn't have such base instincts.

But Logan grinned. "Okay. Go ahead."

"Truly?" I perked up, my tail thumping against the bed.

He laughed a little, petting the fur on my chest. "Yeah,

of course. I only meant that if you kept licking me, the trouble was going to be me getting horny again."

I kissed him. Bless the man for being so accepting of my desires, odd though they may be to him. When he sucked on my tongue, I gave him more of it only to pull back when he choked. But he laughed and rested his hands beside his head, spreading his legs, too.

"Come on then," he said in a sultry tone. "Lick me clean."

With that permission, I let my instinct run free and started by licking his neck. Both sides and from his ears to his shoulders, I swiped at every inch of his skin as I loomed over him. He closed his eyes, fingers petting me wherever he could reach and his every breath letting me know when I found a particularly good spot. Licking over his nipples made him moan. Taking away the come from his belly got him whining with need and growing hard.

Rolling him over, I nibbled along his shoulders and licked the back of his neck a few times. He put his ass up, legs spread wide, and whimpered beautifully, but I didn't give in to the temptation to mate him. I did move down his body, bathing his flanks before spreading his cheeks and licking between them.

Logan started begging me to fuck him again. But I wasn't done licking him yet and I wanted to see if I could make him come just with my tongue.

I rolled him over again and watched him staring at me while I lifted his leg and laved from the juncture of his thigh to the pads of his toes. His cock was leaking on his belly, making me want to clean him, but I treated myself to his other leg first. Logan was stroking himself by the time I finished with his smallest toe.

After licking up the mess on his belly, I removed his hand from his cock and sucked it into my mouth. When he came, I still counted it as a win since my tongue had very much been involved in bringing him off. Flushed pink and panting beneath me, I just stared at him and licked my lips, relishing how very mine he was.

"Come on," he said and hitched his legs back, baring his hole to me. "Take me again."

Knowing he often slept right after sex, I hesitated. But when he licked his finger and then reached down to touch his own hole, my resistance broke. While I grabbed for the lubricant, he moaned at what he did to himself, and said, "Right here. Alam, I need you."

I held his hands over his head and slid so easily into his tight, warm body. It felt like a homecoming, like being buried inside him was where I was meant to be.

As I slowly thrust inside him, Logan squirmed beneath me, eyes closed and lips parted, moaning his pleasure. I could see how much his body wanted him to collapse into sleep, but once inside him I was unable to resist staying there. He'd given himself over to me, and I relished it as a gift.

"Knot," he grunted at one point. "Alam…"

My Logan was a knot-slut, and I was unable to deny him.

I eased it into him as gently as I could and shivered as his throaty moan vibrated through him to me. Something about his barely conscious but so accepting state was all I needed to come deep inside him. He smiled briefly and hummed before his face smoothed out as he finally slept.

Braced on my elbows and knees above him, I tucked my nose against his neck and knew then that I had to answer all of the questions standing in the way of me keeping Logan forever.

All morning long, I couldn't stop thinking of my night with Logan. Bathing him like that had solidified something inside me that had me feeling complete and broken at the same time. It was worry that spoiled my joy. I was worried about what being the heir to the throne and mating a human would mean to mine and my family's future. Would the lack of an alliance mean the end of our reign? Would the lack of an heir do the same?

There was only one way to find out, and I couldn't avoid asking the questions any longer.

Begging off my afternoon of meetings, I sequestered myself in my quarters and put in a call to my mother back on Nor.

"My darling," she said as she appeared on the screen. "How are you? No more troubles, I hope?"

I winced internally since someone had sent word to her about the assassination attempt before they'd known all of the facts. Mother had been preparing a warship to bring her to Earth by the time I'd been able to speak to her. "Hello, Mother. I'm well, and there have been no further… issues."

"Do you call with good news then?" she asked with an eager smile. She and I were of the same dark coloring, while my siblings had taken after our gray father. I liked to think that I would age as finely as she had, with white fur streaking away from her face and making her blue eyes so very bright.

"Of a sort." I cleared my throat and offered up what we'd accomplished yesterday—all of those new businesses—even though I knew I was stalling. It made her smile in a wicked way as I detailed how we were becoming business owners throughout the countries of Earth whether the humans like it or not.

"While I applaud your ingenuity," she said, "I must also caution you."

"I know." I nodded, well aware of the number of messages we had already received from various global leaders asking what we thought we were doing.

"You know many humans won't see this as assistance," Mother continued. "They won't be glad that we found a way to work around their restrictions faster than they might have been able to reverse them. They aren't like us."

I sighed. "Several have reached out. Some with threats. Others to express disappointment. They don't yet see that we are creating jobs in some of the most downtrodden of their communities which will only help those areas to thrive. Jobs for *humans*, I might add. Some of these bureaucrats seem to think our businesses will be staffed by Norlons."

"Hardly," Mother scoffed. "Not if they can't guarantee *your* safety on their planet."

I quieted for a moment, trying to choose my next words and finally tell her why I truly reached out.

"What is it, my son?" she asked. "I can see you're struggling. What's happened?"

I took a breath and just said it. "There is a human male named Logan Parrish. I believe he is my mate."

Her mouth popped open, and she blinked several times. Then her face transformed with a smile, and she pressed her hands to her chest. "Oh, Alam, how happy this makes me!"

I was encouraged by her reaction, but still had to ask, "Does this complicate the future of our rule? I cannot get an heir from him, he does not bring an alliance with—"

"My darling, these are problems with solutions we can find when they are needed." She leaned closer to the screen, her eyes glassy with unshed tears. "I have only ever dreamt of my children finding a love like I knew with Carl. You are blessed."

The weight of my worries lifted in the presence of her acceptance and left me feeling momentarily breathless. She was right that there would need to be discussions at some point and with several advisors to sort out the finer points of succession, but for now, I could celebrate finding my mate.

Oh, and tell him how I felt. I should definitely do that and soon.

Mother wanted to know all about Logan, so I told her what I knew and let her see the human media coverage of him. That he was the one to save me from the assassin made him family in her mind, no hesitation, but she also thought he had a beautiful smile and a brilliant mind.

But in telling her what I knew about him, I realized that there was quite a bit I didn't know. Did he have family? Did he like the idea of leaving Earth to visit Nor? To remain there? Did he even see our relationship as something long term? I ended the call with Mother reassured by her acceptance but concerned that I didn't truly know how Logan felt.

I braced myself and sent a message to him.

> Please come to my quarters at your first availability.

> Absolutely! I'll stop by Halaby's for more cream.

Had we gone through the whole tube already? Before I could feel more than a moment's pride at that, I corrected his impression of what we would be doing when he arrived.

> Logan, we need to talk.

It took several minutes before he replied, making me wonder if I'd interrupted him at a crucial moment during one of the meetings I'd excused myself from. Perhaps I should wait until later in the day? But no, it was done, and we needed to discuss our future...if we had one.

> I'm on my way.

CHAPTER 10
LOGAN

We need to talk. Did Alam have any idea about the fear that little sentence sent through me? I'd stared at those words so long they'd blurred and stopped looking like words. Had I done something wrong? Was it over? I'd wondered if our relationship could last—a prince? with me?—but now I realized I had a serious fear that we *couldn't* last. That we wouldn't be *allowed* to last.

I hated the doubt and insecurities pulsing inside me along with my thundering heartbeat. I had tried to excuse myself from a breakout group discussing the best ways to reassure the parents of sick children that nanobots were harmless, only to have everyone suddenly concerned if I was alright. Smiling, nodding, I had said something else needed my attention and had promised I'd be fine. No one had ever died from a broken heart, right? So I'd survive if he dumped me.

No idea how I got from the conference room to Alam's quarters. Had the guards stopped me? Had I spoken to them? Standing there in front of Alam's door, I suddenly didn't know if I could do this face to face. Maybe if I walked away now, he'd just tell me we were through in a text, and I wouldn't have to worry about ugly crying in front of him. Because, Jesus, I fucking felt like doing just that out here in the hall.

The door opened and there Alam was. He was so beautiful. I remembered back to when the Norlons first arrived, how I'd been scared of the talking animals claiming they came in peace. And now I couldn't imagine a person kinder and sweeter, braver and bolder…who had once been mine. I felt a tear break free and slip down my cheek as I stared up at him.

"Logan?" He reached for me, the pad of his thumb wiping that tear away. "What's happened? What's wrong?"

I swallowed hard and tried to speak as he looked one way and then the other down the hallway. Suddenly, he picked me up under my arms and walked into the room, letting the door shut behind us. I buried my face in the ruff of soft fur at his neck and held onto him. When he tried to set me back on my feet, I wouldn't let him go—I couldn't—so he stood there holding me.

"Logan, talk to me. Are you hurt? Have the humans done something? Did they demand you return to them?"

How could he not know? I might not have ever said the words, but I'd tried to show him that I loved him. Did he need me to say it?

"Please don't let this be the end of us," I said into his furry neck. "I love you, Alam."

He gasped, and then I gasped when he pulled me away and held me in front of him at arm's length. When he set me on my feet, I gulped back a sob as he cupped my face in his hands. "Do you?" he whispered.

I nodded. "I'm sorry if I should've told you sooner, but please don't dump me because I didn't. I'm *sorry*."

"Goddess, Logan." He bent enough to look me in the eye. "I do not understand what you mean about dumping you, but that you love me is everything I wished to discuss."

I gulped, not sure I'd heard him right. "What?"

Alam took my hands and led me over to one of the chairs. Sitting down in one, he had me sit on the coffee table in front of him.

"Logan, I believe you are my mate," he said softly, his eyes kind. "A person so compatible to me that I cannot imagine life without you. I asked you here so that I could tell you this and discover if you might feel the same way about me."

"Oh, fuck." I yanked my hands free of his and covered my mouth as my whole body flashed hot with total embarrassment. I was an overreacting toddler! What the fuck was wrong with me? Sure, every time I'd ever been dumped, it had started with the guy telling me we needed to talk, but… Okay, yeah, that had definitely conditioned me to expect the worst.

But this was Alam…

He smiled at me and rested his hands on my knees. "Will you be my mate, Logan? To love me and stay with me for the rest of our lives?"

That was a marriage proposal! Nodding at him, I really started crying then, just blubbering all over him because I'd fallen forward into his lap. I wanted to answer him, tell him how much I loved him, but I couldn't stop. Amazingly, Alam didn't seem to mind since he cuddled me close and rubbed my back.

I took a huge breath and sat back enough to look at him since he didn't at all deserve to be left hanging like that. "I want to be your mate," I said with a nod. "I do. All of it. I'm sorry."

He chuckled and licked my tear-stained cheek. "Stop apologizing. I worried that you didn't feel the same, but you have shown me I was entirely wrong."

I stopped myself from nodding like a bobblehead and took a few more deep breaths. "I'm not usually such a baby," I said with an awkward laugh as I wiped at my eyes.

"I don't mind," he whispered before his tongue snuck out and licked my cheek again.

Remembering what he'd done with that tongue last night was getting me hard. The twinkle in his eyes and rakish grin on his lips told me he was remembering it, too. Here I was a soggy wreck, and he still wanted me. Alam really did love me.

I kissed him. With his one hand on my lower back and the other on my head, Alam pulled me in close and angled me just the way he wanted me. He licked into my mouth, and I laughed as my much smaller tongue dueled with his. When I felt the prick of his claws against my scalp and one ass cheek, I couldn't hold back my moan and ground my erection against his.

"Stay here with me," he said, his voice a rumble as he undid the closure on my top. "Bring your things and put them with mine."

"Yes." Biting my bottom lip, I let him toss my tunic

away. I was about to say something about moving in together, but he used one claw to open the seam of my pants. The stretchy fabric gave immediately, splitting in half from back to front. My ass was exposed, and my cock and balls sprang free as he smirked at me.

"You ruin a lot of my pants," I said with a frown. "I bet the tailors are going to start noticing."

Alam chuckled wickedly and dragged his claws down the underside of my thighs, tearing stripes into the legs of my pants. I gasped in amazement that he didn't nick my skin even a little and felt my face heat because there was no way the tailors wouldn't know what had happened this time.

"You are so terrible," I said with mock irritation even as I rubbed myself against his still-contained cock.

Alam hugged me to him with one arm and stood up. "You love it."

"Yeah, I do." I licked the corner of his mouth as he carried me to the bed. "You're so proper in public, but here, with me, the beast comes out."

He set me down on the bed and stood back to remove his own clothes—without shredding them at all. The restraint did something hot to me and had me stroking myself as I watched him get naked.

Knowing he was about to claim me, his mate, I said, "Tell me what it'll be like to be your mate."

He smiled as he removed his pants. "You will be prince-consort, and everyone will treat you as they do me. My wealth, my property, my businesses are all yours."

Fuck, that was a lot. "Alam, are you sure you—"

"Yes."

I gulped down what I'd been trying to say because he really was that sure. I wasn't bringing anything at all to this relationship but myself, and he didn't mind one bit.

Naked, he got some lube and slicked his bright pink dick. I drew my legs back and shivered with anticipation.

"What else can I expect as your mate?"

With a wicked grin, he eased his stiff cock inside me. "This is yours whenever or wherever you want it."

"Wh-wherever?" I asked breathlessly.

"Mmm... If you wish my services in the middle of a council meeting, I will send them all away and take you over my throne." He teased my ass with the bulge of his knot, pressing close but not forcing it into me. "Or perhaps you would prefer they stay and watch me take you?"

Holy fuck. I shivered so hard I nearly came. Was exhibitionism a kink of mine? I'd never considered it. But, uh, yeah. Yeah, it might be. I couldn't help moaning as I imagined the scene while the steady pace of his thrusting hips drove me higher.

Alam grinned down at me. "Do you want everyone to know you're mine, Logan?"

I nodded fast because he'd hit on exactly what I liked about letting others see us together. He was also pegging the ever-loving hell out of my prostate. "Yes! Fuck yes."

"And should they also know that I belong to you?"

Oh, that did it! I gasped and came, my breath rumbling out of me in a throaty moan as I gripped my spurting dick and twitched all along his fat cock. He fucked me through it, and goddamn I loved that he did. It meant— Yes! He fucked that knot right up my ass, slamming us together, and binding himself to me. I opened my eyes to see him snarling, sharp teeth bared, as he came deep inside me. I still swore I could feel the heat of him in there and I fucking loved that.

Alam moaned and settled a little more on top of me. He nosed my head to the side and nibbled on my neck, making me shiver. He was always so careful with me, but knowing the threat of claws and fangs were right there beneath the surface added a little extra thrill to our sex. Would he want to bite me? Scratch me? I might let him.

"I should only knot you from behind," he said with a weak chuckle. "I'm trying not to crush you."

He was big, yeah, but not so much so that I couldn't roll us all the way over. The change in position pulled at the knot, but only made us both moan. With my legs hitched up to keep my ass pressed tightly to him, I rested on his chest and relaxed. But then I lifted my head, concerned. "I'm not crushing you, am I?"

Alam snorted. "Hardly." His eyes widened. "You are, of course, quite muscular and strong. Very well built and—"

I laughed and laid back down on him. "Calm down. I like being littler than you."

"Oh. Good."

We lay like that with him slowly petting up and down my back for ages. No matter how much I didn't want to, I felt sleep tugging me away. Before I gave in, though, I just had to say, "I'm your mate."

Alam made a rumbly noise and promised, "Yes, Logan, and I'm yours."

CHAPTER 11
ALAM

No one was surprised by the announcement that Logan and I were mates. Ghosha was particularly proud of himself, as though his words had been what spurred me to finally making my relationship official. And while all I truly wanted to do was plan for the ceremony we would have here—with another on Nor at a later date—I was instead forced to deal with upset human politicians.

Though none of them said so directly, I got the impression that the fact that their constituents praised *us* and not them for the advancements improving their lives was what truly angered the human leadership. We had stolen their moment to shine, to be called saviors. When a reporter on a news show had said we Norlons had cut out the middleman by removing government interference, the American senator he'd been speaking with had left the interview, calling the reporter a traitor.

Humans First rallies were taking place across the globe and their main message was that Norlons would eventually demand payment for what we gave so freely now. They compared us to drug dealers who offered free samples "to get them hooked" only to charge exorbitant amounts once they were addicted. They claimed that we would seduce and steal their young people as compensation for all we gave them.

Combating that perception was the reason everyone had gathered this afternoon. Ghosha was particularly despondent, apologizing for his cavalier behavior and belief that humans would be grateful for the opportunity to work in our brothels on Nor. He was ready to scrap the entire project.

"No, no," I said to Ghosha. "We simply need to pivot and present our facts in a different, more acceptable way."

Beside me, Logan said quietly, "Show them what it's like."

I gave him my attention. "Pardon?"

He blinked at me. Several others looked at him, and I watched his cheeks turn pink as he flicked his gaze to each of them. Did he truly not know how valuable his insights were to us by now?

"What did you say?" I asked him encouragingly.

"Oh, well, I just thought that maybe it would be a good idea to show everyone what working in a brothel is like." He cleared his throat and sat up straighter. "Um, historically, when we did have brothels, they were horrible places full of disease and abuse."

Ghosha made a distressed sound and covered his eyes as he leaned forward on the table.

"But you can change that perception," Logan said urgently. "Interview the sex workers on Nor, the regulators, the... I don't know, just anyone involved in the whole industry, but especially the humans. Make a documentary—a movie—you can distribute somewhere so people can see for themselves what it's like to be a sex worker on Nor."

Goddess, I loved Logan's mind. "You are utterly brilliant," I said before I kissed him heartily.

He huffed a laugh and his blush renewed, but I could tell he was proud to be useful. That it surprised him when others praised his efforts was something I would help him overcome. He deserved to be confident in the fact that he had so much to offer.

"Perhaps," I said, "showing them could be what we do in other areas as well. While our new partners organize the businesses on the surface, we could invite a selection of humans to visit us here and see for themselves what we benefit from every day."

Halaby perked up. "I could take them on a tour of the infirmary. Show them how the nanobots can heal an injury. There are always several small ones each day for one reason or another. Earlier today, we had some crushed fingers when a cargo lift failed."

I winced in sympathy for the injured party but said, "An excellent idea, yes."

Logan said, "I think it'll have the biggest impact, if you could show one of the visitors themselves how it works. I'm still convinced the nanobots I had repaired an old knee injury while they were in there. Maybe we could see about fixing something like that for one of the visitors?"

Halaby grinned eagerly. "That is entirely possible."

"We must choose our guest list wisely," another member of the delegation cautioned. Seiwa Heremod was a Pip with engineering, a genius with anything mechanical, who currently had a small pile of things in front of him that I couldn't begin to name. He seemed to be assembling the bits into a whole while barely glancing at it, long white ears twitching this way and that.

"Agreed," I said. "Though we should allow for both those disappointed in our actions and those excited by them to join us. Perhaps we can change minds."

Logan cleared his throat, and I gave him my attention again. "Um, would it be possible for them to bring a news crew with them? Maybe do a live broadcast? I don't know how the tech works or signal strength from so far away, but if it's possible, then the whole world could watch as it happens."

Before I could turn my head to look at Seiwa, he said, "Let me look into what they're using to do that, and I'll see what I can do to support it. Might be I'll have to get new cameras and whatnot down to them so they can use that." And he said all of that while one hand tightened a screw and the other tapped notes on his tablet. Seiwa's mind must be a chaotic place.

"They'll love that," Logan said with a smile. "Seriously, you'll have every news station wanting in on that event. They might even pay to be the one to do it."

I shook my head. "I would prefer to favor the people who have been the kindest to us, the most supportive of our cause. Bashtine, could you determine which group that is?"

"Of course, Your Highness," she said from her seat behind me. "I will also work on creating a list of potential visitors for you to review."

"If I may redirect us back to creating a film for the sex industry," Ghosha said with a desperate air about him.

With a nod, I agreed. "Of course."

"Logan," Ghosha said, "what does one expect from a... documentary?"

"Oh, well, it's a type of movie we're all pretty familiar with at this point." Logan relaxed back in his chair, looking confident to me. "Filmmakers do documentaries to explore a topic seriously or dive deeper into something. A lot of times, it's an event that was covered in the news, but maybe it was a crime that wasn't solved before the investigators had to move on. Documentaries can expose truths and make a topic more personal for the viewers."

He ended with a shrug, but I was fascinated. We had a thriving entertainment industry on Nor, but it was more focused on fictional stories. Apparently, our news coverage was making documentaries regularly and simply calling it the news.

Ghosha was smiling now. "I believe I know someone on Nor who can help us create a documentary—and quickly. This is excellent. Thank you, Logan."

Logan blushed. "Oh, yeah, you're welcome."

"Would you view a draft of the documentary?" Ghosha asked him. "To give a human perspective on the content?"

"Absolutely. Just, um, keep the sex acts off-screen. Talk about them, sure, but don't show anything." Logan cleared his throat. "That way they'll be able to show it to more people. Regulations and all that..."

I smiled for how shy he was publicly when it came to sexual relations, while being adventurous with me privately.

"Ah, of course." Ghosha nodded eagerly before getting up to confer with the rest of his people.

Quietly, Logan asked me, "How quickly do you think they'll have the documentary done?"

I shrugged but said, "Since Ghosha already knows a professional who might make it, I could see it taking a few weeks or so before you have something to view. Why?"

"Depending on how long it takes to coordinate the visit, you could mention this to the news people you contact. Give them the option to air it, too."

"Yes, wonderful." I made a note on my tablet and shared it with Bashtine since she was busy talking to others.

"This is…" Logan smiled brightly. "This is really exciting. Along with everything else, it feels like we're making awesome progress."

I loved how happy these advancements made him and reached over to hold his hand. "What do you think about also announcing our…engagement?"

That was his word for the state of our relationship, and I liked it. We Norlons were simply mated from the acceptance of the proposal—though the ceremony was meant to celebrate that with everyone—but Logan wanted to label the stage before the ceremony. It sounded far more intimate than I think he realized since he never blushed when he said it.

"Oh, well," he said and cocked his head to the side. "I guess we could. Maybe we tell whichever news outlet that's been nicest about covering our relationship?"

I nodded, unsure which ones had covered the topic at all. "It's possible the same people are covering all things in a favorable light. Would giving everything to them be problematic?"

Logan shrugged. "I don't think so. Everyone else will cover it, and they'll expect that someone will get it first. But a lot of humans have their favorites and will look to them exclusively for the information. I mean, the news people might not like being second, but they're used to it. And really, if they want the scoop, they need to be our friends."

Rewarding the loyal ones made sense to me and I was eager to begin.

"Your Highness?" Bashtine said politely, drawing my attention. "I have the lists prepared." She sent the information to my tablet, and I reached for it.

Logan scooted closer so he could see as well. "Oh, I thought that's who it would be."

"Which?" I asked.

"PBS News. They're publicly funded and kind of on the small side when compared to the other news networks, but they're smart and fair. Maybe more, um, scientifically inclined? They've been around forever, too. Their programming for kids is, like, the gold standard."

I could've happily chosen them based on Logan's feelings toward them, but Bashtine's research also said PBS News was favorable in their coverage ninety-eight percent of the time and when they were critical, it was only to call for additional information so that they might be able to come to a more accurate decision. Their logic pleased me quite a bit.

"These visitors are also excellent," I said to Bashtine. Political figures, yes, but also our helpers on the surface—

lawyers and scientists eager to assist us in bettering the lives of their fellow humans. "Yes, I like all of these suggestions."

"Are we sure about this one?" Logan said, pointing to one name.

I sighed. Bashtine had suggested three names that gave me pause, all of them vocal opponents of us. Mitch Devin, the governor of Ohio, was most vocal about his opinions of our new businesses. Basically, he hated what we'd done, wanted to change laws to prevent us from opening the businesses in "his" state, and though he never said the words directly, I had a feeling he was on his way to becoming a member of Humans First.

"I'm not excited to have him here," I said, "but minds like his are the ones we hope to change by hosting these people and documenting it. Assuming he and the other two accept the invitation, of course."

"Well, then," Logan said with a smile, "let's get started planning this thing."

CHAPTER 12
LOGAN

Moving in with Alam was both exhilarating and making my palms sweat. I'd lived with two boyfriends in my life and while one had ended amicably, the other had really not. I was trying to think positively, not overreact like a child again, and go with the flow. And I reminded myself that I'd never felt for either of those guys the way I did about Alam.

One of the many people who worked for Alam had given me a sort of bellhop's cart and plastic boxes to move all of my things and even offered to do it all for me. I'd insisted I could do it myself since there wasn't that much. I'd had to go on to explain that I liked the process of clearing out one space to go into another when they'd seemed to fret over their prince-consort doing physical labor. Man, were they going to have to change their way of thinking with me.

Alam, of course, was in his doorway the moment I stepped past security. He looked as twitchy as his assistant had been as I walked toward him, my cart rolling along behind me.

"I've cleared drawers and shelves for your things," he said as he backed into his quarters, "but I can have them redesign the space if you need more or something different. I can do the same if you would prefer a different color scheme or—"

"Alam," I said, going over and making him come down so I could hold his furry face in my hands. Him being so awkward was seriously adorable. "I promise, everything's perfect just because we're together."

He took a deep breath and sighed it out, making me have to kiss him. I knew right then, as he rumbled a growl and held me close to kiss me breathless, that I wasn't going to unpack just yet.

"Would you do something for me?" Alam asked when we came up for air.

"Of course."

"Would you mate me?"

For a second, I thought he was asking me to be his mate again. But then I realized he meant he wanted me to top him. "You want… You want me to…" And I seriously made a ring with one hand and poked a finger through it.

Alam chuckled and nodded. "Put your cock in me, yes."

"Right." I cleared my throat. "Um, yeah, okay. Sure, we can…" Suddenly, I was breathless for different reasons. "We can do that."

He frowned, his blue eyes studying me closely. "If you are uncomfortable with such a dynamic, we can continue as we have been."

"No. I mean, if this is something you want, I can absolutely give it to you." I could. I wasn't against it at all. "I just didn't really think you wanted me to top because you're so, you know, dominant and everything," I finished lamely, realizing as I said it that I was stereotyping.

Alam relaxed and combed his fingers through my hair. "I do enjoy it, but not as often as I feel the need to claim you." He licked the tip of my nose, something wicked sparkling in his eyes. "By doing this, I wish for you to claim me in return."

"Oh." Well, shit, that changed everything. Make him mine as much as I was his? "Yeah, I can do that. Fuck yeah," I said on a breathy laugh.

He licked over my lips like he was stealing a kiss before he started getting undressed. I took my time doing the same, watching him more and letting the knowledge that he wanted me to claim him fire my blood. This big, strong, gorgeous person was all mine. Just thinking about that had me pressing a hand over my heart.

Naked, he sat on the edge of the bed and reached for my pants. I danced hastily away, laughing, to save them from being shredded. Alam just grinned wickedly and waited.

"How do you want me?" He licked his lips as his gaze tracked my pants going down.

I thought about that for a moment as I walked over to him. With his hands on my naked hips and mine on his shoulders, I could see some of his tail sticking out along the bed behind him. Did he wag while he fucked me? Because if I took him from behind, that thing could probably knock me over if it got going fast enough.

"Like this," I said and leaned in to kiss him. "I want to see you."

Alam smiled and wrapped his arms around me, lying back and taking me with him. I moaned into our kiss, always loving how soft and thick his fur was against my bare skin. My hands wandered and so did my lips, fingers parting fur so I could kiss and lick at his dark skin as I moved down his strong body.

When I was on my knees between his legs, he shifted a bit so he could move his tail down, letting it hang over the edge of the bed. I eyed it warily but focused on the fat pink cock jutting up from his groin, his knot already beginning to swell. For just a second, I wished I had one so I could give it to him.

"Logan," he rumbled like a plea and thrust his hips up.

Grinning at his impatience, I opened up and sucked the head of his cock into my mouth. A sharp sound jumped out of him, and I lashed him with my tongue. Bobbing on him, teasing both of us with the threat of his knot, I let my hands wander over his thick thighs and the bend of his backward knees. He reached down and lightly scratched at my head, his fingers massaging, his claws tucked away.

I ran my hands up his abs only to pause. *What was that?* I popped off his cock, parted his fur to see charcoal skin, and discovered two dark nipples a couple inches apart on the same side of his abdomen. I sifted through more hair higher up and found another one. With those I already knew were centering his pecs, I realized Alam had a total of eight nipples.

He chuckled. "Did you discover something?"

I rolled my eyes and laughed at myself. "I thought I

knew all the cool things about your body." I tweaked a few of his nipples to make him twitch as he actually giggled. "Surprise!"

Alam grinned and shook his head a tiny bit, like I was ridiculous. Maybe I was, but I did like finding new ways to pleasure him.

While I rhythmically teased two of his tits, I leaned in and licked and sucked at his knot. He made guttural sounds of ecstasy, his hands holding my wrists to keep me where I was. When he groaned and his hips started gently thrusting, sliding his cock against my lips, I discovered a steady stream of precome leaking from him.

Realizing I hadn't brought the lube over, I disengaged from his gripping hands and stood up. Alam whined so loudly and so pitifully, I had to reassure him. "I'll be right back. I'm getting the lube."

He lay there taking deep breaths, and I grinned at how well I'd already undone him. Could I do better? I grabbed the lube, got some on my fingers, and went back to him with it.

Alam watched me while sitting up on his elbows as I eased my slick finger inside him. He was tight, and I felt a shudder work through him as he let me in. I didn't do this very often at all, but man, the feel of him had me wanting to get myself in there as soon as possible. The grateful-sounding moans from him as I added another finger had me biting my lip in anticipation.

"Logan, please."

"You ready?"

"Goddess, yes. Make me yours."

Make him mine? Fuck me, that was what I needed to hear.

Slicking myself up, I moaned too and had to take a moment to calm down. He rumbled a laugh, and I looked up and nodded. "Nearly ended before we began."

Alam smiled like he took that as a compliment, which it was.

Ready myself now, I fit the head of my cock to his ass and eased inside. Fuck, that felt amazing! He swallowed me up like he knew exactly what he was doing, and I just tried not to lose it completely like a total newb.

"Oh fuck, Alam," I practically whined as beautiful heat and pressure stole my mind right out of my head.

Suddenly—and I couldn't quite figure out how—Alam grabbed me up and flipped us over so that he was on top. With one of his hands holding both of mine by the wrist over my head, he fitted us back together and fucked himself on my cock with a deliciously brutal pace that had me wailing. Alam snarled down at me, his other hand stroking his cock just as fast as he bounced on mine.

I was done. I should've been able to go way longer than that, but holy fuck, he never gave me a chance. He was a beast of lust demanding satisfaction, and I was absolutely helpless to resist him.

I came with a slam of my hips up into him, body straining against his hold on my arms, and an ecstatic scream caught in my throat. But when he came, his cock shooting all over me, he threw back his head and howled like a wolf. The triumphant sound and the feel of him spasming on my dick had me shuddering in awe as I gasped for breath.

With no knot to tie us together this time, Alam scrambled off of me and blew my mind all over again when he started frantically licking me clean. His long tongue slurped up every trace of his come from my flushed and panting body while he made little whining noises. I had to grab his fluffy, pointed ears to stop him and make him kiss me, letting me taste that filthy tongue of his.

Eventually, I found myself cuddled up with his cock tucked between my legs and one of his thighs caging me in. I just smiled into the fur of his neck as he held me and sighed like everything was perfect.

It really, really was.

It took a few days to get everything set up for the humans to visit, and I seriously couldn't get over that. Days. Not weeks or months. The guests, news crew, and tech for that crew to broadcast live from space was all ready to go in three days. I would've thought no politician would ever act so quickly or that anyone could rig up the tech that fast. But the politicians had cleared their schedules immediately, and Seiwa—that big white rabbit-looking guy from engineering—had slapped a device of his own making onto the side of the news crews' cameras on the ride up from Earth, upgrading them in an instant.

I stood beside Alam as we all waited for the shuttle to touch down in the landing bay. It was open to space at the moment, so we stood on the other side of a clear wall until the hangar doors closed and the room pressurized. Of all the tech the Norlons had, forcefields weren't something they used because they weren't that eco-friendly—apparently, even aliens were conscious of the importance of being green.

That I was standing *beside* Alam was a new thing since our engagement. Normally, I would've stood behind him, back with Bashtine and other consultants and assistants. But now that I was the prince-consort, I was considered to be an equal to Alam in rank. Really only a few little things had changed—like where I stood—but though the people I worked with regularly remained as friendly as ever, they did things like call me "Your Highness" too. The first person to do it had been Bashtine, and I'd corrected her, only to have her give me a look like she thought I was just too precious before she said it again. It was going to take some getting used to.

I wasn't feeling any pressure—at least not any new kind—but I think maybe I stood a little taller and I had definitely developed a regal wave and head nod. I was trying not to be too much of a douche, though.

A quiet horn sounded, and Alam gave my hand a little tug. I walked with him into the landing bay as the shuttle's ramp finished dropping down. I was desperate to look calm, cool, and collected since I'd been in a room with some of these people before, but having a camera pointed right at me was really unnerving. At least it was Bashtine handling all of the introductions, so I just had to stand there, smile, and shake a few hands.

The only people I really knew were Mayor Jacoby and Captain Lewis, my former boss, and they were both eager to say hello and ask how I was doing.

"Since the ship has gravity," Jacoby said, "you won't

have any of that weakening muscles and bones stuff happen, right?"

Lewis perked up at that. "Like astronauts on the space station do? I remember reading about those twins."

I wasn't sure what twins she was referring to, but I shook my head and laughed a little. "I mean, I still need to work out and all that, but I'm not wasting away thanks to the awesome food they have up here."

I wanted to tell them about my engagement, maybe see how they felt about it before our planned announcement over dinner tonight, but some older man in a suit started hollering. At first, I thought he was freaking out over being up here in space on a ship—I could sympathize with that. And then I heard him.

"We're not going to let our way of life be corrupted by these invaders!" He ripped open his suit coat to reveal a vest covered in—

I didn't think, just grabbed Jacoby and Lewis and dragged them with me as I ran toward Alam. He wasn't that far away. I could reach him.

"Bomb!" I yelled.

People started screaming and running, but that didn't drown out the man's final words.

"Humans First!"

The explosion lifted me right off my feet and sent me flying.

CHAPTER 13
ALAM

A concussive force had me hurtling backwards, my head snapping against the floor when I landed. I'd heard Logan yell, heard that human's words, but confusion still had me sitting up in a daze. Then I blinked and I saw.

I couldn't hear them over the sound of klaxons, but the anguish on the faces around me told me they were screaming in pain and terror. Logan was quiet as he got back on his feet, and I could've cried for how calm he was as he directed two humans ahead of him. My unshakable mate. He walked toward me, a hand out, and I reached for him.

Leaning close, he spoke directly into my ear. "Are you hurt?"

I shook my head, but then I winced.

The alarms stopped suddenly, and I flinched at the sound of panicked and pained yelling from everyone around me.

"Guide them out," Logan said firmly. "Get everyone who can go with you out of this room."

I nodded at him, glad for the direction, and stood up. I was somewhat unsteady and nauseous, but if Logan wanted me to leave the bay, I'd go and take as many people with me as I could.

"Come," I said, waving at the two people who had been with Logan. "This way."

The sudden barking words of Captain Langarus startled me, but they were reassuring right afterward. Like Logan, Pysina was calm and in charge. That he was closer to the shuttle concerned me and that he held an unconscious human man against his chest was even more troubling. They were both clearly injured, yet Pysina controlled the room like the seasoned leader that he was.

As I herded Bashtine, the two humans, and a few others toward the exit, a stream of emergency personnel began rushing in through it and several other doors around the bay. We hadn't brought security in—goddess, we'd been so foolishly trusting—but they were here now with several medics.

I allowed myself to be guided out and into the cargo hold opposite the landing bay. It seemed they were going to use it to assess our injuries because I was encouraged to sit on a box of some type before the medic with me peppered me with questions.

"I need to see Logan."

"Your Highness, you're bleeding. Did you hit your head?" The pale gray pads of the Khess's fingers were dotted with blood.

I shook my head but then nodded. "I think I did. I'm dizzy and have a headache."

"Possible concussion," he said to another medic who handed him a syringe. "With your consent, Your Highness, I'd like to—"

"Yes, please. I need to be clearheaded." I reached for the other medic and snagged the Pip's arm. "Please find Logan."

She nodded and hollered my request to someone else. I tried not to be annoyed that I wasn't being obeyed immediately, but my heart was racing with worry for him. Just because he'd been fine when he'd spoken to me—

"Ow! Fuck," I groused as the Khess jabbed the syringe of nanobots into my upper arm.

"Apologies, Your Highness. If you'll just—"

"Alam!" Logan was suddenly in my face, his eyes wide and worried. "You're bleeding!"

"I'm fine. They're fixing it."

Logan looked to the medic while I focused on touching my mate. He had a bruise on his cheek and bits of detritus in his hair.

"I've given him an injection of nanobots," the Khess said, "to combat a possible concussion. They will also repair the wound to his highness's head and any other injuries."

"They're not focused on one thing?" Logan asked. "They'll get anything that's wrong? Honey, please," he said to me as he took hold of my hands. "I'm okay."

I couldn't help the whine that left my throat as I flexed against his restriction, needing to touch more of him.

"Okay. It's okay." he said and leaned into me, tucking

his face into the ruff of fur at my neck. He relaxed against me, and I could finally breathe as I held him.

As the minutes ticked by, I calmed but also became more aware of everything happening around us. The wall of the cargo hold in front of me had been opened and so had that of the landing bay, allowing more people to pass through on both sides, but also letting me look back in at the destruction.

The shuttle our visitors had arrived on was torn apart and there might be a hole in the floor of the bay. It wasn't open to space or anything so catastrophic, but it was still highly concerning. Could we even use the landing bay to send the other humans back to Earth?

But more disturbing was the number of bodies being removed from the bay. They were carried out via a different set of doors, but so far, I had counted six—four humans and two Norlons. That there had been deaths sliced a hole into my heart.

Logan sat back and gazed at me sadly, reaching up to wipe the tears from under my eyes. "It'll be okay," he whispered. "I know it's terrible now, but we're fine and we'll help everyone get through this."

I couldn't stop my self from glancing back into the bay as another dead Norlon was carried away. But that was also when I saw that the human news crew were still filming. They looked broken and singed, but they continued to point their cameras at everything that was happening around them.

"They're filming," I said, not sure what I thought about that.

Logan looked before refocusing on me. "Let them. The people of Earth need to see what's happened."

"Won't they see it as a success? I heard what he said."

Logan held my face in his hands and looked me in the eyes. "I have to believe there are more decent humans down there who'll condemn what he did and cry out for justice. I have to believe that, and you should, too."

I nodded and kissed him gently.

"How are you feeling now?" he asked as he petted the fur of my cheeks.

"Better." Which meant I needed to do more than sit here with my mate. I didn't want to move. I wanted to find a soft place to hide away with him and pretend none of this was happening.

"Come on," Logan said and urged me to stand. "Let's go see where they need us."

The guilt settled on me when they asked me to speak to the ship about what had happened because Pysina was in the infirmary. Those directly beneath him wanted to take some responsibility off of his shoulders even though he continued to bark orders while the medics worked on his injuries. I had agreed, but my guilt was heavy.

"I don't know what to say to them," I admitted to Logan, the only person I'd wanted in the conference room with me while I prepared. "All I can think is to apologize for doing this to us all."

"Christ, no." Logan came over and sat on the table in

front of me, taking my hands in his. "*You* didn't do anything to anyone. That murderer Devin who blew himself up did this. He's to blame, not you."

"But he was here because of me."

"No, he was here because of *me*."

"What? No!"

Logan sat back with a shrug. "I'm the one who suggested we show them what things are like. The documentary about sex workers on Nor? If I hadn't suggested that, you wouldn't have thought of bringing people up here for a tour."

"That's not the same thing," I insisted. "You're not to blame."

He gave me a small and patient smile. "And neither are you."

Damn his logic. By my way of thinking, I could place blame on a whole host of people who hadn't thought of the possible trouble or noticed something was wrong. All of us would've been culpable if that was true.

I slumped back in my seat. "You're right. My guilt remains, but you are right."

"Then maybe this will help."

Logan held up his tablet so I could see the human news coverage on the screen. There were two people, a polished woman I didn't know and a soot-covered man who was one of the crew members with us. They were discussing the footage of the aftermath of the explosion while it played behind them both. It was clear each of them had cried at some point.

With a swipe of his finger, Logan changed to another station that was covering a growing group of people gathering outside of an official-looking building. Some held signs—

"They're protesting Humans First?" I looked to Logan for confirmation even though the newsperson said exactly that.

"Yeah, they are," he said with that smile. "As bad as this all is, it's gotten people on our side in a big way. They may have been fine with ignoring people who were angry about something—that happens all the time—but now that it's gotten violent, now that people have been killed, they're standing up to call for justice and demanding authorities classify Humans First as a terrorist organization."

Terrorists… We hadn't had anything like that on Nor for several generations, not since they had made guaranteed income and universal healthcare available to everyone. For a moment, I felt superior to humans. But truly, I just wanted them to stop fighting each other and us.

Logan set his tablet down and got himself straddling my thighs. "Do the ship-wide announcement. Reassure everyone that they're safe and the ship is fine. Tell them the visiting humans are being investigated and supervised. And then let them know that the people of Earth are rising up in our defense."

Thankfully, the address wasn't intended to be visual because I held Logan to my chest with one arm and the mic in my other hand. When I heard the tone to begin, I spoke from the heart.

"This is Prince Alam Ye Lena speaking on behalf of the delegation to thank each of you for your swift actions and professional dedication as we work through this painful time. While we mourn and repair, know that the humans of Earth are protesting the faction that hurt us and demanding their leaders take steps to condemn it. Though their enlightenment has come at a heavy price, I believe now that they see us for what we are: a people who are determined to raise them up to our level of comfort and safety. I have not changed my course, and I hope you have not either." I paused to cuddle Logan closer. "Seek out and accept assistance where and when you need it as you move through your grief. We are all here for you."

I ended transmission, and received confirmation that it was cut from the tech who had set it up in Communications. Setting down the mic, I wrapped both arms around Logan and just held him.

"That was good," he said into the fur of my neck.

I nodded, rubbing my cheek on his head. "If you need to speak with a counselor, know that we have several available."

"I'm okay with this kind of therapy at the moment." He sighed against me, and I agreed that holding my mate was all I needed for now as well.

CHAPTER 14
LOGAN

Funerals were a universal event. The ones we held on the ship for the Norlons who'd passed in the explosion weren't that different from any I'd attended for humans back on Earth. Religious folks led prayers in Norlish that appeared on the tablets of anyone who wanted to follow along in English and other languages. Captain Langarus said kind words about his crew members.

It was a somber day of mourning that had most of us gathering in small social groups or spending time alone. I stayed by Alam's side because the both of us were still dealing with the guilt of it all. I knew I shouldn't feel responsible about anything that had happened, but the guilt wasn't easy to shake.

After extensive questioning of all the human visitors, the only one who was a little less free to move around the ship was a kid named Owen. He was the son of Mitch Devin, the governor who'd tried to kill us all. I got that Owen might be one hell of a suspect on paper, but it was clear to me that he hadn't had a clue what was going on with his boss. But Owen was pretty much glued to a member of the crew night and day, and I wasn't convinced it was a punishment when he was with Captain Langarus. The authoritative Lago seemed to have a thing for Owen, and I was pretty sure it was mutual. They were, after all, sharing the captain's quarters for no reason anyone could figure out.

Once the repairs had moved along enough to make the landing bay serviceable again, the Norlons had arranged to send the human casualties back to Earth. I thought it was promising that none of the survivors wanted to leave then, choosing to continue on with their original purpose instead. That helped me fight back the guilt because they wanted to be there—they cared to learn. It took a couple of days for us all to reset, but we carried on with our original plans for tours and Q&A sessions with various members of the delegation and their departments.

That all of it got to be broadcast to the surface was also really good. Support was growing by leaps and bounds, especially when the businesses the Norlons had set up slowly started opening across the globe. Workers cut ribbons, crowds cheered, and reporters followed up with those benefiting from the services for nanobots, generated food, and purified water.

It was all so encouraging. But what really got me out of the funk I'd been in was when Alam looked over at me from his chair and said, "We should have our mating ceremony soon."

"We should?" I'd been getting dressed, pants on but tunic in my hands. "It's only been a week."

Alam nodded. "It would lift the mood of everyone on the ship, give hope to all, and…" He shrugged, looking a bit sheepish. "We could take advantage of the favor being shown to us by the humans now and possibly have much less ire to wade through."

He might feel weird about taking advantage of the situation, but I didn't. I could absolutely see the good in tapping into what we had going for us. Our relationship status popped up now and then when the PBS news crew caught us doing something like holding hands or leaning close, but it wasn't the story. Most of the time, people seemed curious more than they condemned us—but that could just be because of the bomb and people not wanting to get lumped in with the terrorists.

I went over to sit on the coffee table in front of Alam. "You don't think they'll change their tune once they know exactly what's going on with us?"

He shrugged and waved on hand. "Possibly, but I don't want to live my life on whether something will be well-received." He smirked and leaned forward to run his big hands up my thighs. "I want to mate you because it's right for us."

I shivered at his touch and grinned at his words. "You know, you use 'mate' in a lot of different ways."

"Mmm yes, but each way means the same thing." He licked the tip of my nose as I took his furry face in my hands. "Mating you makes you mine."

"Fuck, I love that." I used my grip on his cheeks to pull him in for a kiss.

Alam took hold of my waistband and tugged, and I obligingly lifted up so he could take my pants down over my ass. He was getting better about removing my clothes instead of shredding them. I still lost at least one piece a week, but that was an improvement.

Bare-assed on the coffee table, I kept kissing Alam as he encouraged me to lie back. Once I had, though, he stood tall and got himself undressed as if he valued his own clothes more now, too. Or maybe he just liked how I watched him and stroked my cock while I did. Probably that.

Then Alam was leaning against me, his wicked tongue licking and sharp teeth nibbling at my neck and shoulders while his hands wandered. I pulled his hips down and rocked our cocks together, loving the soft sensation of his fur on my skin and the promise of getting knotted soon.

A sudden crack made us pause.

Alam pulled back to look me in the eyes. "Was that the table?"

Before I could answer that it might've been, he lifted me up and stood. I looked down and winced because there was a huge crack in the glass of the tabletop. Literally from one side to the other and exactly where I'd been laying. It might've shattered with a little more time and pressure.

Alam set me on my feet and turned me around to face away from him. He ran a hand down my back, and I realized he was checking to make sure the glass hadn't cut me.

"There's only one crack on me," I said with a wiggle of my ass, "and it's always been there."

He laughed and palmed my butt cheek before I watched him go get some lube. Man, I loved how his bright pink cock stood out from the midnight fur of his body—it was so beautifully obscene. As he walked back over, I made the decision to stay right where I was, spreading my legs and putting my hands against the wall. I felt like I was about to get frisked in the naughtiest way.

A moment later and Alam dropped a wooden box at my feet. "Stand on that," he said and took my hand as if to help me up.

It took me a moment to realize that I was too short for him to fuck me while we were both standing—I needed a lift. And hey, that meant we hadn't done it like this before, which helped ease the little bit of embarrassment as I stepped up onto the box.

The fact that he immediately started teasing my hole with the head of his cock took away any other thoughts on the height issue.

"This is my favorite," Alam rumbled near my ear.

"Wha— What is?" I asked because there was a lot going on at the moment that was making me love this. He was ever so slowly thrusting his way into me inch by inch while clawed hands held my hips and his breath fanned down along my back, telling me he was watching himself fill me.

"Mating you from behind," he said. "Seeing how you so readily take me into your tight, hot body. The way you shiver and pant as I fill you. I swear you were made for me, Logan."

I nodded, believing that wholeheartedly. I'd always preferred receiving, but it was so much better with Alam. Physically, he gave me more sensations than I could keep track of between his long, thick cock, his fur, and his claws. And let's not forget that knot—I fucking craved that thing. Even now, as he worked himself all the way inside me, I felt the bulge of his knot bumping my rim and wanted nothing more than for him to stuff it into me.

"I… I'm yours."

Alam hummed in agreement and wrapped his arms around me. One went high, his fingers poking his claws in a circle around my left pec. The other went low, his big hand closing around my cock. He didn't stroke me, just held on, like he was claiming it as his.

I could've come just like this, but then Alam started thrusting with more force, faster and deeper. Each one had his knot teasing me, and I tipped my ass up and rocked with him, begging without words for him to fill me completely.

He had me pressed against his arms, pinned to the wall, and with my head turned the way it was, I could see him start to snarl as he got closer to his release. Fuck, I loved seeing the diplomatic prince sizzle away to reveal the ravenous beast beneath the surface. All those dangerous teeth, two sets of fangs, and the growling… Oh, fuck, I was coming!

Alam was too because he shoved in hard, forcing me to take his knot. I wailed as my rim stretched with that perfect bite of pain. His hand on my cock squeezed just right and his claws threatened my pec, every sensation just too much to resist. My knees buckled, but Alam was leaning on me now and I wasn't going anywhere as his cock pumped me full of his come and his knot locked it inside me.

I shivered and moaned, no doubt making an absolute mess of the wall, and swore I could feel the heat of him inside me. Whether that was possible didn't really matter because I just loved knowing I was absorbing a little more of him each time he fucked me. Maybe I was becoming Norlon by injection.

Eventually, Alam peeled us off the wall and walked over to sit down in his chair. I moaned at the way the position jostled his cock inside me and let myself collapse on top of him. I had my eyes closed until I heard him licking something and opened them to find Alam cleaning his fingers of my come. When he realized I watched, he aimed his finger at my mouth.

I opened up and accepted his come-covered finger. Rolling my tongue around it, I also sucked rhythmically.

Alam huffed a small laugh. "That certainly isn't going to help relax my knot," he said as he took his finger back.

I smiled, not telling him that I wouldn't mind round two starting with him already locked inside me.

As I lounged there on him, just basking in the bliss, I realized I hadn't answered him about the mating ceremony. I also knew there was nothing I wanted more than to publicly declare that he was mine.

"Let's have the mating ceremony soon." I rested my hands on top of his on my belly and twined our fingers. "Do you think we can do it in the next week or so?"

Alam rubbed against my cheek. "If I tell them to make it happen, they will."

"Give the order, Your Highness."

He lifted our joined hands and kissed the back of mine. "I love you, Logan."

I smiled serenely and closed my eyes. "I love you, too."

Whatever came next for us and the entire delegation, I knew we'd make it through just fine because we were together. We could do anything that way.

THANK YOU FOR READING!

I sincerely hope you enjoyed reading Alam and Logan's story as much as I loved writing it!

If you would be so kind as to write a review telling other readers why you liked this book, that would really help me. As an independent author, reviews are super important to my success.

Please leave your review for *Knotted by the Wolf Prince* at Amazon.

For a sneak peek at Chapter 1 of *Claimed by the Fox Captain*, turn the page!

CLAIMED BY THE FOX CAPTAIN
CHAPTER 1

CAPTAIN PYSINA LANGARUS

I blinked at the ceiling, my heartbeat and breaths loud in my ears. Why was everything red? Then it was as if my ears popped because I could suddenly hear far too much. Klaxons wailed, the blaring alarms beating out every other sound and making me tuck my ears down to try and escape the hideous noise. And that was when I remembered what had happened.

A bomb. One of the humans had detonated a bomb strapped to himself. He'd screamed something about Humans First and then tried to kill us all.

As captain, I wasn't able to escape any of this. I was in charge.

My back protested as I sat up, a sharp pain shooting down to my left knee, but it was the human who slumped from being against my chest to into my lap that truly concerned me. *Friend or foe?* But since the lean young man was unconscious, his intentions didn't matter much at the moment.

I cupped the back of the man's head and felt for a pulse at his neck. Strong and steady. Maybe the explosion had thrown him into me and knocked him out. He didn't smell like a threat—he actually had a very pleasant scent. Reassured for now, needing to engage with the recovery efforts, I held the man close to my chest and stood up.

A quick look around showed me security and medical personnel rushing in and doing their assessments. Commander Sorke sprinted toward me, and I pulled him closer when I couldn't hear a single thing the Lago said.

"Shut these damned alarms off!" I nearly screamed into Sorke's round ear.

Sorke nodded and ran off, leaving me to hope he knew where the controls were. I knew my ship but not every button and switch. Blessedly, it was just seconds before the klaxons quit their screeching.

But in the quiet, now I could hear the cries and moans of the injured and dying. My heart constricted in horror and sympathy as the security personnel and my own commanders gathered around me, awaiting their orders.

"Security, support the medics. Have them triage everyone in the cargo hold. Open the doors completely so there's easier access." They rushed off as a horrible thought occurred to me. "The royals! Has anyone seen—"

"There, sir," Sorke said beside me, and I followed his pointed finger to where Prince Ye Lena and his new prince-consort were standing. I took a steadying breath and refocused.

"I need every human checked for weapons, even the bodies. And get me a damage report. Are the bay doors holding?" I looked to the damn things, willing them to hold even as I saw some part of a shuttle embedded in one side like a knife.

"Engineering is on the way," Lieutenant Commander Rigger, a tall gray Yook, said before he too cast a worried glance at the doors.

I nodded at that. "Someone get on the bay's main control panel and keep an eye on the atmosphere in here. I want to know if there's even the slightest loss of pressure."

"Yes, sir," Rigger said before jogging away.

"Once the bay is clear, we seal it off as if there's been a breach. I want no chances taken here."

"Yes, sir," the rest of them said.

"Go!" I barked when they didn't move. "Check the humans and get that damage report."

They scattered, but at least they looked like they knew where they were going. As I watched them go, I saw Seiwa Heremod jet around the room like his fuzzy white tail was on fire. As head engineer, this had to be one of his nightmares, but he was calm and focused even as he leapt from place to place near the shuttle.

As I watched him, I realized there was a hole in the flooring. Thank the goddess the explosion had gone down into another cargo hold instead of up into crew quarters—third shift would've been in their bunks at this hour.

"Sir?" a Lago medic said as he approached me. "Is he alive?"

I blinked at him in confusion. "Who?"

"The human you're holding."

I looked down, alarmed and even more confused to find that I still held the skinny man against my chest, one arm looped under his and hugging him tightly to me. I hadn't noticed. I hadn't meant to carry him with me.

"I… Yes, he's alive. Just…unconscious."

The medic was nodding as he approached like I might fight him off. "Can I take him? I'll evaluate him right here."

Why was my first instinct to turn away and deny him access? That didn't make any sense. A medic wanted to help an injured person. I shouldn't prevent that.

"Of course," I said and stepped closer to the medic. "You can take him."

He did and eyed me cautiously while he eased the human into his arms and laid him on the floor at our feet. There were things I needed to do, but I stood there watching the medic evaluating the human instead. I couldn't make myself look away.

"He has a severe concussion," the medic said up to me. "Should I treat him now, or wait for him to be conscious enough to consent?"

He shouldn't have even asked me, and I knew what I should do, but I didn't hesitate to say the opposite. "Do it now."

The medic nodded and prepared a syringe. I couldn't stop the growl that left me when he stuck it into the man.

"I apologize," I said when the medic looked up at me.

"It's alright, sir. I understand."

Did he? Why didn't I?

"Now let's see to you." The medic stood and moved around behind me.

"There's nothing wrong with me." Except for the fact that I needed to pick the human up again and was trying to resist that urge.

"You're bleeding, sir."

I followed his pointing finger to see a small pool of blood under my left boot. "Fuck," I said as the pain suddenly registered. I made to reach back, touch where it hurt, but the medic grabbed my wrist to stop me.

"There's a piece of something embedded in your lower back. Just be still for me." He let my wrist go and came around in front of me again, scanning me with one of his devices like he'd done with the human at my feet. "I need a gurney!" he yelled over his shoulder.

"I can walk," I protested, but the instant I tried to, my left knee buckled like it wasn't even connected to the rest of my body.

The medic caught me under my arms, and I couldn't help the yelp that left my throat as the sudden move pulled at whatever was stabbing into me. I wanted to reach back and rip it out of me, but even the pain didn't let me forget how badly I might bleed if I did.

A moment later and two more medics arrived with gurneys, the three of them settling me on one and the human on the other.

"Keep them together," my medic told everyone.

I wasn't sure if I wanted to ask what he knew as I kept my gaze on the unconscious young man being pushed down the corridor beside me.

Reserve your copy of *Claimed by the Fox Captain* direct from Delaney's store for a 10 March 2024 release or via Amazon for ebook and KU release a week later.

ABOUT THE AUTHOR

Delaney Rain is an author of M/M paranormal romances featuring supernatural creatures and the men who love them.

Come for the GRR
Stay for the AWW

Read Chapters on Patreon
https://www.patreon.com/delaneyrain

ALSO BY DELANEY RAIN

FURRY ALIEN MATES

Knotted by the Wolf Prince

Claimed by the Fox Captain

Bound to the Tiger Scout

Captured by the Dragon Warrior

Hooked on the Otter Doctor

DELANEY'S SEA MONSTERS

The Sea Monster's Mate

Aquaculture Affair

DELANEY'S BIGFOOT

The Bigfoot's Mate

For Fur's Sake

Double Bigfoot Trouble

DELANEY'S INCUBI

The Incubus's Mate

Friends of the Incubus's Mate

DELANEY'S DEMONS

The Demon's Mate

A Death Worth Living

STANDALONES

Tentacles and Other Stocking Stuffers

The Demon's Dealbreaker

The Aliens' Mate

The Red Dragon's Mate

The Unicorn's Mate

The Minotaur's Mate

FEATURING PROWL'S *IS IT OUT THERE?* SHOW

The Red Dragon's Mate

The Demon's Mate

For Fur's Sake

Double Bigfoot Trouble